Yours for the Holiday

by

Erin Bowlen

Any resemblance to persons living or dead is purely coincidental.

Copyright © 2022. All rights reserved.

Cover Design by Tugboat Designs

Table of Contents

Chapter One 1
Chapter Two 19
Chapter Three 35
Chapter Four 56
Chapter Five 79
Chapter Six 104
Chapter Seven 119
Chapter Eight 137
Chapter Nine 147
Chapter Ten 160
Chapter Eleven 178
Chapter Twelve 187
Chapter Thirteen 193

Chapter One

Los Angeles, California

Ally Hayes weaved her way through the crowds of Christmas shoppers on Rodeo Drive.

"Excuse you." She artfully avoided a collision with a man carrying several shopping bags, yelling into his cellphone, who was completely oblivious to her presence. So many people pressing in around her made her feel slightly claustrophobic as she swerved to avoid being hit by another passerby. It didn't help that the weather today was particularly warm – well, warm for her compared to the cold Canadian winters she was used to. Despite living in Los Angeles for the last six years, she'd never quite adjusted to Californian weather. Slowly pushing her way through for another block, she found herself outside of the café where she was supposed to be meeting her friend, Liv Daniels.

"Could I just squeeze through here? Thanks." She made her way through a small group of people standing out front.

"Hey!" one of the twenty-something hipsters protested as she pushed her way to the front of the line. Ally ignored them.

"Can I help you, Miss?" the maître-d' asked her with a who-do-you-think-you-are look for cutting the line.

"My friend is just at that table over there." She pointed to Liv, who waved at her.

The maître-d' glanced over at Liv, who looked every inch the leading actress she aspired to be with her smooth, brown skin with its bronzed glow, her warm, reddish-brown eyes, full lips, and the graceful posture of a ballet dancer. He then stared at Ally, who looked, well, less like the leading actress she aspired to be and more like the Irish peasant farmers her ancestors had been with her dark brown hair, bluish-green eyes, and pale, peaches-and-cream complexion. From his expression, she could tell that he was confused why someone so glamourous was hanging out with her.

Same, buddy, same, she thought. She chose not to be insulted by his bafflement. After all, it was a mystery to her as well why Liv had chosen to be her friend, but she'd been grateful for that friendship every day since she'd moved to Los Angeles. Without Liv, Ally probably would have packed up and left for home with her tail between her legs long ago.

Still, he lifted the rope that barred the entrance and let her onto the patio outside the café, much to the protests of those still waiting in line.

"Thank you," she told him politely and hurried across the patio before he changed his mind.

Yours for the Holiday

"Sorry! Sorry!" she exclaimed, grabbing the empty seat across from Liv. "I know. I'm late. These crowds are nuts!"

"I know, right? It's like it's almost Christmas or something," she joked.

"Speaking of Christmas, how excited are you that in less than a week, you and Jackson are going to be on a romantic ski trip to Vermont?"

A blissful look crossed Liv's face at the thought of her upcoming trip away with her long-term boyfriend. "I can't wait for it! I need a vacation so bad right now. I just wish I didn't have to worry about you being here by yourself."

Ally waved her hand, dismissing her concern. "No, don't be. Just because Tom and I broke up and I'm no longer going to Maui for Christmas doesn't mean that you need to worry about me."

Liv gave her a look like she seriously doubted that.

"Really, Liv. Tom and I... we just grew apart. I'm fine with it. You don't need to worry about me." Ally buried her head in her menu so she wouldn't have to meet her eye. The truth was, it still hurt that she wasn't going to be going away for Christmas like she'd planned, while Liv got to go away on this super romantic trip Jackson had planned for her, but when Ally realized she was more upset about not going to Maui than she was about the fact that she and Tom had broken up, she knew it had been the right thing for them to split up. Still, she was grateful when the server arrived a few seconds later to distract Liv for a few moments.

"Can I take your orders?" he approached them, interrupting their conversation.

"Do you know what you want?" Ally asked as she

contemplated the menu.

"I'll have a water and a green salad. Dressing on the side."

"And I'll have the same," Ally replied. The server took their menus and disappeared off towards the kitchen.

"Let's talk about something happier. Do you think Jackson is going to propose to you on this romantic trip he's got planned?"

"You know, you never really told me what happened between you and Tom," Liv changed the subject.

"It's like I said: we grew apart."

Liv leaned back in her chair, crossing her arms gracefully across her chest.

"What's that look for?" Ally asked, feeling scrutinized.

"The old 'we grew apart' statement? That's the excuse celebs use when they don't want to tell people the real reason they broke up."

Ally rolled her eyes. "Ok, how about the 'we wanted different things' excuse? Specifically, he wanted to work on his career, not on our relationship."

When she thought back on her four-year relationship with Tom, their break-up had kind of been like a sad denouement. Surprisingly, for two actors, their break-up hadn't had much drama: no shouting matches, no throwing his clothes over the balcony. It had all been pretty civilized. After he'd come home from his latest film set, they'd just decided one night that things weren't working as they were, and so they'd agreed to end it. No fuss, no muss.

"And what about you? What do you want?" Liv asked her.

"Hmm?" She was broken out of her reverie.

Yours for the Holiday

"You said that the two of you broke up because Tom wanted to work on his career, but what do you want?" It was an excellent question, and not one that Ally had a ready answer to.

"I don't know," she admitted. "I'm not sure what I want."

"Well, how do you feel? Sad, angry, disappointed, happy, relieved?" Liv probed.

"I don't know that, either. I know I should say that I'm sad, or devastated, or whatever, but I'm not. Does that make me a terrible person?"

Liv smiled at her and reached across the table to squeeze her hand. "Of course, not. You could never be a terrible person."

Ally felt a sense of relief wash over her. "I guess I feel... disappointed, maybe?"

"Well, that seems only natural. You two were together for four years. But, anyway, I say screw him. Work is definitely not more important than you."

Ally smiled at her. "What would I do without you?"

"I honestly don't know," Liv replied smugly.

Ally didn't know either. She'd come to Los Angeles just after her high school graduation with absolutely no idea about the world, only a dream to be a famous actress. She'd been lucky on her first day in the city when she'd seen a flyer outside of her hostel for an acting class that was being held in the basement of a church a few blocks away. It was there that she'd met Liv, this self-confident, mid-western young woman a few years older than her, that had moved to Los Angeles to pursue the same dream. Liv had already spent time learning how to navigate the pitfalls of the acting industry, and she'd kindly taken the naïve Ally under her wing.

"We ladies need to stick together in this industry," Liv had told her on that first day they'd met. "So much of this industry is about pitting you against other people and seeing how you survive, but I think the real lesson we need to learn is how to work together. Where you staying, by the way?"

Ally had told her about the hostel.

"Oh no, not that rat-infested place. I stayed there my first week, too. You're coming to stay with me until we can get you a place of your own."

And from that day forward, Liv had been true to her word. She'd helped Ally find an affordable place to live, had gotten her set up with some acting classes, and even got her in front of her agent so that Ally would have representation. She'd shown her everything she'd needed to know about getting into the acting industry, and she'd done it all, expecting nothing from her. When Ally had asked Liv about this one day, she'd countered with her a question of her own: "If you were in my position, would you do the same for me?"

Ally hadn't even had to think about her response before answering. "Yeah, actually, I would."

"Well, there's your answer, then. I told you; we've got to stick together. The world needs more people helping other people out." Ally found she couldn't disagree with that philosophy and the two of them had been firm friends ever since.

Back in the present day, the server returned with their salads.

"Here we go," he said, placing their plates in front of them. They both thanked him before Liv turned her attention back to the conversation at hand.

"So, what *are* you going to do for Christmas if you aren't going to Hawaii? You can't stay home by yourself

Yours for the Holiday

and lonely like some Bridget Jones movie."

"Who says that I'd be lonely?" Ally felt a bit piqued at having been called out. She had, in fact, planned on sitting in front of the TV with a tub of ice cream and a bottle of vodka, and watching a bunch of romantic Christmas movies, pretending that she hadn't just broken up with her boyfriend two weeks before Christmas. Hawaii and opening presents on the beach had never seemed like so much fun right now.

"Umm... every Hallmark movie ever written," Liv teased her. "Ally, everyone who's alone at Christmas is lonely. I mean, is there anything worse?"

"Landslides, earthquakes, tornadoes..." Ally started listing. She was trying to be humorous, but even she could tell she was doing it more for herself than for Liv.

"Fine, fine," Liv conceded. "So, I'm exaggerating. *Again*. Whatever. I just don't think you should be alone at Christmas. I'd totally invite you to spend it with me and Jackson, but the chalet in Vermont is only a one-bedroom, and to tell you the truth..."

"You don't really want me there?" Ally offered, smiling at her so that it didn't sound harsh. She would've been lying if she'd said that she wouldn't have minded being taken in for the holidays, so she wouldn't have to be alone, but she also knew she couldn't impose on Liv and Jackson's big holiday. It was the first time the two of them had decided that they weren't going to either of their parents' places and were taking a holiday for just the two of them.

"No! It's not that at all!" Liv looked hurt that she would think that.

"No, you're right. This could be the trip where Jackson proposes to you. I mean, he booked this whole totally romantic week away for you in Vermont, of all places. It's a fact that all the best Hallmark movies are set in little towns on the East Coast like the one you're going to. If he doesn't do it now, then he's a total idiot." In truth, Ally knew Jackson did, in fact, plan to propose to Liv on this trip because he'd asked for her help in picking out the ring, which was another reason she was not going to impose on them this Christmas.

Liv smiled excitedly at the thought. Ally knew how much it would mean to her to get engaged at Christmastime. Ally would have been lying if she didn't say that the thought of someone else getting engaged at Christmas stung more than a little, even if it was one of her closest friends. It wasn't like she'd thought Tom was going to propose to her on their trip to Hawaii, but just knowing that it *wouldn't* happen now for certain, well, it all just kind of sucked.

At just that moment, her cell phone rang, bringing her out of her maudlin thoughts. She turned her phone over and saw "Mom" on the caller ID.

"You need to get that?" Liv asked her, expectantly.

"Nah, I'm sure it's just my mom asking if I'm coming home for Christmas this year." She clicked "Decline," and let it go to voicemail.

"Well, there's an idea!"

"What?"

"Well, if you don't have anywhere else to go for Christmas…" Liv shrugged her shoulders like maybe she should consider it.

"I'm not *that* desperate, Liv!"

"Oh, come on. What's so wrong about going home for the holidays? I mean, you actually *like* your family."

Yours for the Holiday

Ally was close to her family; she and her mother and sister talked to one another almost every day, but she felt a sense of trepidation at the thought of actually going home.

"I just don't want to deal with the questions," she confessed. "You know: 'Where's Tom?' 'Why haven't we met him?' 'Why did you two break up?' Or worse: 'How's acting going?' 'Got any roles yet?' I mean, I love my family, but it's humiliating to go home without a boyfriend and without a shred of success to my name. Everyone back home will think I'm just some colossal failure."

"Ugh, those questions are so annoying!" Liv agreed. Ally knew Liv related to the feeling all too well. She'd been asked the same questions when she went home to Minnesota, too. "But I don't think they're going to think you're a failure, hun! The right part is just around the corner for the both of us. I can feel it."

Ally smiled at her. It was impossible to feel sorry for oneself for too long with Liv around.

"Speaking of, how do you think that audition went?" The two of them had recently auditioned for an upcoming rom-com their agent had sent their way. Liv had gone for the lead role, while Ally was hoping for the supporting role.

"I don't know... I hate to jinx it, but I think it went well?" Ally got nervous just thinking about it. She loved acting, but she hated auditioning. She especially hated waiting after the audition to see if she'd gotten the role. All that pent-up anxiety drove her mad.

The two of them finished their salads and talked some more about work until their lunch date had come to a natural end.

"Well, it was so nice to see you before we leave for Vermont." Liv rose from her chair and leaned over to kiss Ally on both cheeks as they got ready to depart.

"Don't forget to call me if Jackson happens to, you know, pop the question." Ally gave her a knowing look.

"You'll be the first to know," Liv promised. "And don't forget to call your mother and tell her you're going home for the holidays."

Ally rolled her eyes. "Fine, I promise to call her first thing tomorrow."

"You're going to call her right now on your walk back to your apartment." Liv's tone was firm.

"Alright, alright." Ally pulled out her cell phone to prove that she meant it. "I'm dialling her right now."

Liv waved to her as she walked back to her car. "See you on New Year's Eve!"

Walking back to her tiny apartment, she couldn't help but think how unnatural it was that Los Angeles was so green and sandy during the winter. She was used to east coast Canadian winters, where the wind would blow right through you and chill you to the bone. It was weird to say, but all this sand and sun made her feel more depressed about the upcoming holiday. It was like California was mocking her with its cheeriness and perpetual summer. She pulled out her cell phone and listened to her phone messages.

"Hello, dear. It's Mom."

"Like I didn't already know that," she muttered mirthfully to her voice messaging machine.

"Anyways, I wanted to call to say that your Grams had a fall."

Ally felt her heart drop for a moment. She'd always been close to her maternal grandmother, and the thought of something terrible happening to her made her feel sick to her stomach.

Yours for the Holiday

"She's ok now."

Thank God! She felt a wave of relief rushing over her, her mind having gone to the worst things her imagination could think of.

"She didn't want to worry you and make you come home, but we decided it would be better if she didn't live alone anymore. I know you said that you and Tom were going to Hawaii this Christmas, but I think it would be really nice if you came home to visit her for the holidays. It would really cheer her up to see you. She's a bit sad at having to move into the seniors' home right before the holidays."

Even though her mother had said her grandmother was fine, Ally couldn't help but be worried. She hung up her phone and video messaged her little sister to find out more.

"Cass!"

"Hey Al. How's sunny L.A.?"

"Oh, you know... sunny... sandy... the usual."

"Only you can make that sound like torture," Cassie joked, playfully sticking her tongue out.

"What can I say? It's a gift," Ally joked. "Anyways, Mom called me."

"Uh-oh, giving you the annual guilt trip because you haven't been home in forever since you decided to pursue your acting dream? How *is* that going, by the way?"

"Don't you start!" she snapped, even though she knew Cassie was only kidding. "I had an audition last week for a very promising supporting role in this upcoming rom-com, if you must know."

Cassie was suddenly serious now. "That's great! I'm so proud of you!"

"Thanks, Cass," she smiled at her. "Anyways, I

wanted to call because Mom said that Grams had a fall or something?!"

"Oh that." Cassie waved her hand dismissively.

"Yes, that! Why didn't you call to tell me as soon as it happened?" Ally was feeling a bit put out that she'd been left out of this really important family news.

"You know Grams; she didn't want a fuss, and she didn't want to make you come all the way back home from L.A." Cassie shrugged her shoulders, like Ally was making a big deal over nothing.

"Still, you should've told me!" Ally pouted, her mouth making a perfect moue, like she had been taught in her acting classes. "And Mom says that she's depressed at living in the new nursing home."

"Pfft! She loves it there! She's made a ton of friends and she's happy as a clam."

"So, she's ok?" Ally persisted, needing to hear the words again, just to be sure so she could stop worrying.

"Oh yeah, she's fine. Mom kind of freaked out a bit, though; you know how she is about these things. Anyways, she didn't like the thought of her being on her own anymore, and so she and dad moved her into a home. She's doing fine, I promise you."

"Well, if you're sure that I don't need to come home…"

"I'm sure we'll all be fine if you don't come home. You'll be missed, of course, but we'll understand if you want to stay somewhere sunnier and warmer than here."

"Well, ok…" Ally was suddenly distracted by someone she saw through the window of her local bakery she walked by.

Oh no! Not him! She ducked her head down. The last person she wanted to run into now was Tom.

"Cass, I have to go."

Yours for the Holiday

"Wait... Ok... Bye, I guess," Ally heard her sister say as she hung up and tried to walk on by.

"Ally?"

She turned around at the sound of her name, trying to appear surprised.

"Tom! I didn't see you there." Ally put on her best smile, trying to pretend like this was not about to be really awkward for the both of them. Out of a city of twelve million people, of course she would run into him. It was like Fate was conjuring him up after her conversation with Liv earlier. "So... what brings you to this part of town?"

"I had a sudden urge for those pains au chocolat we used to get. You remember the ones?" he asked, nodding towards the display case through the window.

"Of course." Every weekend, the two of them would come here to Sami's Bakery without fail and indulge in their cheat day treats. It was their special spot. Even though she wouldn't admit it to him, she'd had brief moments of nostalgia since their break-up and had come by the bakery in the half-hearted hope that she might run into him again. When that hadn't happened and she was just about to give up, now here he was. It was just like him: he always showed up just when she was about to call it quits with him. The long weeks and months spent apart while he away on film sets had made her doubt from time to time whether the two of them should be together, and just when she'd think about breaking up, he'd pull out some romantic gesture that would make her forget for awhile why she'd wanted to break up in the first place. It was partly why they'd lasted as long as they had.

She was just about to make a polite excuse and head back to her apartment when a leggy blonde supermodel arrived and linked arms with Tom.

"Hey, lover," she crooned.

Ally stood there, astonished. She knew Tom wasn't the kind of person who would end up being single for long. Even so, knowing that he'd already moved on with someone only a couple of weeks after they broke up was like a knife in the heart.

"Hey." Tom's whole face broke out into a smug smile. He pulled her in close and the two of them proceeded to have a mini make-out fest. Just when Ally was beginning to think they might've forgotten she was standing there and she should just slip awkwardly and quietly away, they finally broke their embrace.

"Ally, this is Tamara," he said, gesturing to the blonde. "Tam, this is Ally."

Tamara gave her a look, sizing her up, and clearly, Ally was falling woefully short of whatever expectations she'd had of Tom's ex-girlfriend. It uncomfortably reminded her of how the maître-d had done the same thing to her earlier.

"Hi," Ally smiled, trying to appear friendly, given how awkward this was for all three of them. Tamara seemed unimpressed by the gesture.

"Hi," Tamara returned, her tone curt.

"Tam's a model," Tom said, making conversation.

"Oh. Nice." Ally wasn't surprised. She was too perfect to be anything but a model.

"And Ally's an aspiring actress," Tom supplied. Tamara stared at her in disbelief.

God, I hate L.A. sometimes, Ally thought to herself. *Does everyone have to size me up all the time?*

"Oh. Nice." Tamara repeated Ally's sentiment.

Trying to find some kind of common ground with her ex's new girlfriend, Ally noticed the shopping bags

Yours for the Holiday

Tamara was holding. "Been doing some shopping?"

"Yes," Tamara suddenly glowed. "Tom's taking me to Hawaii for Christmas, and I wanted to pick up some new bikinis before we go."

Hawaii for Christmas. The trip that Tom was supposed to be taking her on this year. She had to admit, it stung more than a little to know that he was taking his girlfriend of less than three weeks on the trip the two of them had been planning for months.

"Hawaii? Oh, wow. How nice." She glanced at Tom, who had the grace to look embarrassed by this conversation. Ally was pleased. He deserved to squirm a bit.

"Do you have any big Christmas plans?" Tamara asked.

Ally felt uncomfortable under the other woman's smug gaze. From the way she was looking at her, Tamara clearly thought she was going to be sitting at home by herself, pining over Tom. Ally's mind froze for a moment, then zeroed in on the one thing she'd recently been thinking about.

"I'm going home to Canada. Yeah, my grandmother fell the other week, and I thought I'd come home to surprise her as a Christmas gift."

Even though she'd been insistent to Liv that she wasn't going home for Christmas, she'd been right; there was no need for her to be alone and lonely in Los Angeles when she could be at home with family.

"Oh, I'm so sorry." The words were kind, but Tamara's tone hinted that she was bored now and really couldn't care less about Ally's grandmother.

"Yeah, sorry to hear that," Tom repeated while glancing around, seemingly looking for a way out of this conversation. It was clear to Ally now that he'd only approached her so he could show off his shiny new girlfriend, show her that he'd been the first one to move on. Tom had always been competitive. It was what had made him so good at auditioning and getting the roles he wanted. It was why he'd just called her an "aspiring" actress, even though she'd had some minor roles throughout her career so far. He was trying to diminish her work because she hadn't been as successful as him yet. He'd done that throughout their relationship: dropped more than a few hints that she needed to be more like him when it came to auditions if she wanted to get better roles. He tried to get her to come out with him all the time to parties where executives, producers, and casting agents would be, even though he knew she hated those kinds of events.

"You need to put your face in front of them over and over again, so they don't forget you," he'd told her. Ally, meanwhile, had focused on honing her craft. She didn't like the schmoozing part of the job like he did.

"You know what, babe? We should probably get going. You said you wanted to hit up some more stores before we head home. It was nice seeing you, Al. Have a Merry Christmas."

He whisked Tamara away before she could say anything, and the pair headed down the street in the opposite direction. Ally sighed and stepped inside the warmth of the bakery.

"Hey, Sami!" she greeted the middle-aged Tunisian man who owned the place.

"Hi, Miss Ally!" He gave her a huge smile. "Haven't seen you here in a few weeks. Did you get your big break yet?"

"No, not yet," she sighed. "But I just had an audition that I'm hoping will lead to a big role."

"Well, I hope you get it," Sami smiled at her

again. "I just saw Mr. Tom come in here a few minutes ago."

"Yeah, me too," she muttered. Sami seemed to pick up on her mood.

"Go and have a seat," he told her. "I'll bring you the biggest hot chocolate."

"Thanks Sami. Have I told you that you're my favourite person?"

"Not today you haven't," he teased her before going to get her drink order. He came over to her table a few minutes later with a big mug of hot chocolate and a few fried doughnut-like desserts.

"Bambalouni," Sami said, placing them in front of her. "Tunisian doughnuts. And it's on me," he told her when she tried to bring out her wallet to pay him. "You look like you could use a… what do the Americans say? A pick you up?"

"A pick me up," she smiled, correcting him. "Picking someone up is a different thing entirely, and I'm really not sure Mira would approve." Ally waved to Sami's wife, whom she could see through the kitchen door.

As Sami turned to greet a new customer, Ally brought out her phone again and called her sister.

⁕

Cassie picked up her phone when she saw her sister's name come up on the caller ID.

"Yeah?"

"Cass, tell Mom and Dad I'll be home for Christmas."

"Um… ok." Cassie wasn't sure what had made her sister change her mind about coming home in the last ten minutes, but she could tell from the look on her face that she didn't want to talk about it. "Well, we'll be happy to have you! Video chatting just isn't the same."

"Then it's decided. I'll be on the next flight out!"

"Oh! There's just something I should warn you about the place where Grams is staying…" Cassie started.

"Whatever it is, Cass, we can talk about it when I'm home. Gotta go! Gotta book my flight! Bye!" Ally abruptly hung up the phone, leaving Cassie to stare at her phone screen.

"What was that about?" her mother asked, walking into her room with a laundry basket full of clean clothes.

"Ally's coming home for Christmas."

"That's great news! Isn't it?" she asked, seeing the look on Cassie's face.

"Um, yes. It's just that she doesn't know that Chase works at Grams' nursing home, and she hung up before I could tell her."

"*Oh.*" The look on her mother's face said it all.

"Yeah. Things are going to get real interesting when she finds out."

Chapter Two

Fredericton, New Brunswick, Canada

The small plane landed with a bump on the tarmac at the Fredericton Airport. As she deplaned, Ally was hit with a rush of freezing cold air and she wrapped her sweater tighter around her. Since living in Los Angeles, she'd gotten rid of all her winter clothes and was, therefore, totally unprepared for a true Canadian winter. She raced across the tarmac and hurried inside the airport to get out of the cold. Standing by the luggage claim was Cassie, who was holding a sign that read: "My Sister's a Famous Actress!"

She beamed at the sign and her sister.

"Welcome home!" Cassie squealed, causing some fellow travellers to look in their direction, startled by the noise.

"It's great to be back." She pulled Cassie in for a tight hug.

"C'mon, Mom has a huge "welcome home" meal cooking for you and I'm starving!"

Ally laughed at her. "It's a good thing that I haven't eaten anything since the panini I got before leaving L.A.X, then."

They picked up her luggage from the carousel and headed out to the car for the thirty-minute drive to their childhood home. As they crested Brick Hill – sensibly named for all the brick houses that once belonged to the cotton mill workers who once lived in them – and began the steep drop into Marysville, Ally couldn't help but stare at the spectacular view of the nineteenth-century cotton mill village she'd grown up in. Marysville was as pretty as a postcard at any time of the year, but it was especially beautiful in winter with its old architecture and the snowy banks of the ice-covered Nashwaak River running through the centre. Ally was always surprised that it still hadn't been the setting for some Hallmark movie yet.

As they turned down the street at the bottom of the hill and pulled into the driveway of their parents' two-storey brick house, Ally felt a sense of relief at coming home.

"Ally!" Her mother threw open the front door and wrapped her arms around her eldest daughter.

"Mom!" she protested as her mother pulled her into a bear hug and smothered her with kisses. "I can't breathe!"

"Let her get in the door, Mary," her father playfully chided his wife, who reluctantly let her go.

"Yes, please! It's freezing out here!"

"Well, no wonder; you're not even wearing a winter coat!" her mother chastised.

Yours for the Holiday

"It's not like it ever gets cold enough in L.A. to need one," Ally pouted, pulling her sweater tighter around her.

"Well, come on in and let's find you something warmer to wear. Your mother's been cooking up all your favourites today."

"Food!" Cassie exclaimed, pushing past her father and sister, promptly dropping Ally's suitcase in the front hall, and heading straight for the kitchen with singular purpose.

Ally laughed.

"Where's Grams?" she asked, peering over her father's shoulder into the living room.

"She was feeling tired earlier, so she decided to stay at the nursing home. She said to say that she's looking forward to seeing you tomorrow, though."

Ever since she'd heard her mother's voicemail, Ally had had this unshakeable feeling that there was something that her mother and Cassie weren't telling her about her grandmother's condition.

"Tell me the truth, Dad. How is she doing?"

While Cassie and her mother might understate the seriousness of her grandmother's condition, she could always count on her father to tell her the truth.

His dark blonde brows drew down a bit, thinking. "Well, when she fell, she banged up her hip pretty bad, so she's quite sore, but thankfully she didn't break anything," her father was quick to add, seeing the look on her face. "She also hit her head, and it's led to a bit of confusion from time to time, but the doctor said that this could also just be her age. The doctor's primary concern right now is that the fall seems to have been caused by a heart condition that causes her to get light-headed. This is why we wanted her to move into the nursing home, so someone would be around to keep an eye on her, and she'll get immediate attention if anything does happen."

"Well, that makes me feel a bit better," Ally admitted. "Not the part about her falling or the heart condition, but that she's not going to be alone the next time."

"She'll be ok." Her dad patted her on the shoulder. "Your grandmother's a tough old bird. Reminds me of a few other women in this family." He nodded first in her direction, and then toward her mother and sister were bringing out the plates for supper. Ally felt pleased at the compliment. She couldn't think of anyone she'd rather be compared to than her grandmother.

"Hurry up! What's everyone waiting for? Let's eat!" Cassie called from the kitchen.

"C'mon, let's get in there before your sister eats everything on us," her dad winked at her.

Ally followed her father into the noisy kitchen, warmed by the contented feeling of being home.

☙❦

The next morning, Ally heard the sounds of her mother getting breakfast ready in the kitchen directly below her childhood bedroom. Her mother, knowing that both her daughters were easily motivated by food, had often chosen to wake them up throughout their teenage years by cooking them a big breakfast every morning. Ally and Cassie could both easily sleep through the irritating buzzing of their alarm clocks, but neither of them could stay asleep once their stomachs started rumbling.

Ally turned over onto her side and opened one eye, staring blearily at the time. She sighed; in Los Angeles, it was still the middle of the night.

Yours for the Holiday

"Wake up, sleepyhead. Smells like food's on the table. Do you want the bathroom first, or do you mind if I go?" Cassie asked, popping her head through her open doorway.

Ally grumbled something incoherent into her pillow.

"What?"

"I said, 'I'm pretty sure this whole time difference thing is going to kill me,'" Ally repeated herself, this time lifting her head from the pillow.

"So, does that mean I can go to the bathroom first, then?"

"Fine. Sure."

A few minutes later, Ally heard her sister leave the bathroom, and she reluctantly rose from her bed, walking zombie-like through her morning routine, and headed downstairs for breakfast. The scent of homemade blueberry pancakes and maple syrup wafted from the plate her mother set in front of her.

"Eat up," she commanded. "You've gotten too skinny since moving out to L.A. We need to put some weight on your bones again."

Ally stuck her finger into a dollop of maple syrup, savouring the taste. "Mmm! It's so good to have the real stuff!"

"Don't they have maple syrup down in the States?" Cassie asked.

"They do, but it's just table syrup. Tastes nothing like the real stuff."

"Heathens," Cassie joked, appalled by the idea of replacing pure maple syrup with table syrup. They tucked into their breakfasts, lightly chatting about their plans for the day.

"As soon as we're done here, I'd like to head over

to see Grams. Mom, do you mind if I borrow your car?"

"I can take you over. I was planning on visiting her today anyways," Cassie said.

"Don't you have a class today or something?"

"Nope. Finished exams last week. I'm free as a bird until next term." Cassie breathed a sigh of relief at being done with her university work.

"Cool."

Twenty minutes later, they were dressed and ready to head out the door.

"Wow, this place has grown up," Ally marvelled as they drove towards the nursing home in the neighbouring suburb of Devon. When she was growing up, this entire area had been a forest. Then, just before she went to high school, they'd built Leo Hayes High School where she and Cassie had gone. Then had come the Willie O'Ree recreation centre, named for the NHL's first black hockey player, who was from right here in Fredericton; then Two Nations Crossing, and so on and so forth.

"Look at the school!" As they drove by, she noticed how there were now mobile classrooms added to the distinctive horseshoe-shaped building.

"Yeah, it's bigger now than when we went there," Cassie agreed, turning down the street towards the seniors' home.

Ally had loved her time at the school. It was where she'd gotten up the nerve to follow her acting dreams. What she'd loved most about it had been the yearly musical productions where her love of acting had turned into a passion. There was only one thing that marred her happy memories of that time…

Ally didn't want to dwell on Chase, though, as she and her sister had pulled up to their destination. Still, she couldn't help herself from thinking about him yesterday when she'd landed on her parent's doorstep and saw his childhood home next to hers. Like it or not, he'd been on her mind since she'd decided to come home.

"Hey there, Grams!" Cassie greeted their grandmother cheerily as they entered the rec room. "I've got a surprise for you!"

"Oh? What's that?" her grandmother asked, perking up a bit with excitement.

Ally felt her breath catch in her throat at the sight of her maternal grandmother. She still looked much the same as the last time she'd seen her, but there was a frailness to her now that hadn't been there before. Ally could see the bruises on her arms where she'd tried to break her fall, the ones that her long-sleeved shirt couldn't quite hide. Even though they'd begun to fade, it still made Ally worry.

"Hey there, Grams." She pushed aside her worries and put on the biggest smile she could muster as she leaned down to give her a kiss on the cheek.

"Ally!" Her grandmother beamed up at her, her voice breathless. "What a lovely surprise! Did you come all the way over from Los Angeles just to see me?"

"You betcha!"

"Well, isn't this the best Christmas surprise?" She took her Ally's hand in hers, her skin feeling cool to the touch. "Everyone, this is my granddaughter, Ally Hayes. She's going to be a famous actress," her grandmother proudly announced to the group of elderly ladies who were sitting at the game table with her. Ally smiled warmly at each of them.

"One of these days, I'm going to move away so I can be the favourite granddaughter," Cassie mumbled.

"Now, now. You know I don't play favourites with my granddaughters," Grams admonished her. "You are going to be a brilliant social worker one day, Cassie. I've no doubt about that. You're going to help a lot of people who need it, and I'm just as proud of you as I am of your sister. Now, Ally. Come meet my new friends."

Ally obliged by moving closer to the table.

"This here's Ruth, Dorothy, and that one there trying to cheat at Scrabble is Helen."

"I was doing no such thing," Helen protested, looking up from the little wooden block letters she'd been rearranging on the board before her.

"I saw you moving those pieces around when you thought I wasn't looking."

"I was just trying to see if my word would fit in there," Helen replied defensively. "So, you're a famous actress, then?" she asked, changing the subject and turning the attention away from her.

"Well, not just yet, I'm not," she politely corrected her grandmother's earlier statement.

"Well, you had that make-up gig, didn't you? Your mom showed me a photo of you in a magazine. You looked very pretty."

"Thanks, Grams, but that was just a bit of modelling. It wasn't really an acting job…"

"Ally's always been the prettiest girl in town, hasn't she, Grams?"

"Well, look who finally showed up to work!" Her grandmother turned slightly in her chair to get a better look at none other than Chase Cormier.

Ally felt her stomach plummet to the floor.
Oh God.

Chase Cormier, former high school baseball star, the male lead in every high school musical production, the prom king to her prom queen, and Ally's ex-high school sweetheart, whom she'd dumped on prom night, was standing right next to her. She'd known when she'd come home that there was a possibility that she'd run into him. Even though there were fifty thousand people in this city, this was still the Maritimes, and everyone knew everyone, and the chances of avoiding him had been miniscule.

So awkward. This is so awkward. So, so, so awkward, was all Ally could think. *God, how was it he'd gotten even more handsome in the last six years?*

He'd trimmed his longish, light-brown hair into a style that was less like a nineties boy band wannabe into something resembling the current fashion, and he'd grown a beard, which made him look more impossibly handsome than before. But those dark brown eyes, so dark as to almost be black that he'd inherited from his Mi'kmaq grandmother, had remained the same.

Ok, so repeatedly saying the word "awkward" over and over in her mind may not have been the *only* thing she could think of.

"Ally Hayes. Long time, no see. It's good to see you." He extended a hand towards her, and she felt herself go through the motions of shaking it. His grip was firm and warm, his fingertips calloused.

"Hey." *Hey? Come on Ally, couldn't you think of something better to say to your former best friend, the person who knew you best in the world, the guy you were once madly in love with?*

"What are you doing here?" She hadn't meant it to sound rude. "I just mean… um… this isn't exactly the kind of place I'd expect to see you hanging out at."

Smooth, Ally. Real smooth. She could feel her subconscious facepalming at her complete lack of game in this moment.

"I work here. I'm a music therapist." He seemed amused by the look of confusion on her face. It hadn't been what she'd been expecting him to say at all, but when she stared up into those dark eyes that seemed to see right to the very depths of her soul, she saw he was being serious.

"Wow, that's... that's pretty cool." She didn't know what she'd actually expected him to be doing here, but it certainly wasn't that.

"Yeah, the dream of becoming a famous baseball player kind of went by the wayside when I broke my collarbone that summer after high school," he admitted. "Then, my grandmother, you remember her?"

"Of course." Chase's maternal grandmother, Pauline, had been living with Chase and his family in the house next to the Hayes' ever since they were kids. Pauline had been of Mi'kmaq ancestry and had spent many a lazy summer day with Chase and Ally, telling them the legends and stories of her people, who had once been the caretakers of the land they now all lived on. Ally had always fondly remembered her for her kindness, a trait she'd instilled in her grandson.

"I was so sorry to hear that she'd passed away. I meant to call..."

Chase gave her a half-smile, to let her know she was forgiven, another trait he'd picked up from his grandmother. "When I got to university, her Alzheimer's got worse, and suddenly, I just wanted to do anything that I could to help her keep her memories for as long as she could. So, I did some research into it and found that music therapy had been proven to help with cognitive recognition, so I switched career paths."

She marvelled at how grown up he seemed. While Ally had always known that she'd wanted to be an actress, Chase had always been a dreamer, bouncing from one career idea to another. Because he was so infuriatingly good at whatever he tried his hand at, it had made settling on a particular career even more difficult.

"I still do some coaching, but just for the fun of it," he was telling her as she brought her attention back to the conversation at hand.

Of course, he coaches little league, she thought. *Of course, he'd still be perfect at everything.*

"Wow, that's great." Ally didn't know why, but she still couldn't seem to form a coherent thought – or sentence – when she was around him. She was relieved when Helen interrupted the awkward exchange.

"Chase, dear, could you come here for a moment?"

"Duty calls." He smiled at her and excused himself.

"Well, that was like watching a train wreck," Cassie's voice cut through her thoughts. "Like, I couldn't decide if I should look away or not, but it was just too entertaining *not* to watch you look like a complete idiot."

Ally glared at her ferociously.

"Why didn't you tell me Chase was working here?" she hissed at her younger sister.

"Um, I *tried* to tell you when you called me from L.A and said that you were coming home, but you hung up on me, remember?" Cassie corrected her.

"No, obviously I don't remember, otherwise I wouldn't be asking," Ally retorted.

"Well, I did, and I tried, and you're welcome."

"But you didn't do anything!" She wanted to scream at her sister, who was now walking away from her, just as Chase returned.

Oh God, just make this day end, she thought to herself.

"Sorry about that. So…" he started.

"Been a long time," she finished his sentence, resigning herself to having this awkward conversation with him.

"Yeah." He smiled at her, and she involuntarily felt her insides do a few somersaults. She was suddenly very aware of her body: what should she do with her hands? Should she put them in her pockets? Leave them by her side? Fold them across her chest? The latter, she noticed, emphasized her chest area, and immediately dropped her hands to her sides. She'd raided her old high school clothes for something warm to wear and found this crimson V-neck cardigan, which was a touch deeper than she'd remembered.

"Yeah, it has." A distant look fell across his face like a shadow, like he was thinking about the last time they'd seen each other, their prom night, when she'd told him they had to break up because she was moving to Los Angeles, and he'd tried to talk her into staying.

"How long are you in town for?"

She noticed he seemed just as confused about what to do with his own hands, before watching him finally settle on putting them in the pockets of his jeans. She felt a sense of relief that he felt just as awkward as she did right now. Her thoughts then drifted to the way his stance pulled his long-sleeved shirt tighter across his chest and accentuated his broad shoulders, and she tried her best to forget what it felt like when those arms used to be wrapped around her.

"Just for a week. I'll be back in L.A. for New Year's," she replied, tearing her eyes away from his body.

"Oh."

She couldn't help but notice the hint of disappointment in his voice. She wasn't going to lie; a small part of her was thrilled. Looking around the room for some kind of distraction, she pointed to a stack of boxes taking up the centre of the room. "So, what's going on here?"

"That's for the Christmas Eve dance," a young Syrian girl of about ten piped up, seemingly appearing out of nowhere. She came over to stand by Chase, joining their conversation. Ally watched as Chase's whole countenance changed, becoming more relaxed around the young girl, and his face took on an almost fatherly look of pride.

"Ally, this is Fatima. Fatima, this is my old friend, Ally."

"I recognize you from Chase's pictures!" Fatima smiled warmly at her. Ally smiled back at her infectious enthusiasm. "You're the actress, right? Grams showed me your photo in that magazine you posed for. You're really pretty. Isn't she pretty, Chase?"

Chase's cheeks flushed beneath his permanently tanned skin. "Yes, she is."

Ally felt her own cheeks getting warm at the compliment. "Thank you."

"The Christmas Eve dance was Fatima's idea," Chase supplied.

"Yeah, not everyone can be home with their families for the holidays, so I wanted to cheer them up," Fatima interjected. "So, I thought it might be nice to have a dance for everyone, so they don't have to feel alone. And we're going to sing Christmas carols. And we're also asking people to bring donations for the Food Bank."

"Wow! That's a really sweet idea. That's really thoughtful of you."

"Thanks." Fatima smiled proudly. "You know, we could use some help with it. I bet you know something about party-planning. You must go to loads of fancy parties in Hollywood." Her tone was dreamy.

"I've been to a few," Ally replied noncommittally. She didn't want to shatter the young girl's dreams of the Hollywood lifestyle, but her life there was far from glamourous. She and Liv had snuck into a couple of Oscar after-parties, but most of their time was spent at home with a bottle of wine and a good movie when they weren't in acting class or auditioning.

"You wouldn't happen to be free sometime this week and happen to, maybe, want to help us out, would you?" Chase managed to look both shy about asking and hopeful that she'd say yes at the same time. "It's totally fine if you don't. Have time, I mean. Or want to help out. You're only home for a short time; I'm sure you want to spend as much of it with friends and family as you can."

"*You're* her friend," Fatima pointed out. "So, helping out with the dance counts as spending time with friends.

"She has a good point," Ally conceded. She liked the thought that she and Chase might still be friends after all these years. "Um… let me check my incredibly busy schedule," she teased, playfully pulling out a pretend work diary.

Fatima giggled.

"I'm sure I can squeeze in some time for you." Ally winked at her. "When do we start?"

"Does tomorrow work for you? I can come and pick you up on my lunch break?" Chase offered.

"Nah, that's ok. I was planning to come over and see Grams for a bit tomorrow anyways, so I can meet you here. Say, about one o'clock?"

"It's a date. I mean…" he looked mortified. Fatima smirked at the Freudian slip.

"Sounds great. I meant to say that, that sounds great. We should probably go now. Come on, Fatima."

Yours for the Holiday

He steered the young girl toward a few elderly ladies who were vying for his attention at another table. "We don't want me to get fired right before Christmas, now, do we?"

Ally smiled and waved farewell to Fatima as they headed across the room. As weird as it was seeing Chase again, and as awkward as things had started out, she felt a little disappointed that their conversation was ending so soon. In some ways, it had been like no time had passed between them, but at the same time, it felt like a million years since she'd last talked to him. He was the same old familiar Chase, but also different, somehow. More grown up. She definitely didn't feel like the same could be said about her. Her eyes lingered on him a moment as he and Fatima walked away.

"Careful now, dear. If you stare at him longingly like that, your face will freeze that way and give your thoughts away."

Ally jumped a little as her grandmother spoke, bringing her back to the present moment.

"I don't know what you mean." She felt her pale cheeks getting redder.

"Chase and Ally sitting in a tree," Cassie chanted. "K-I-S-S-I-N-G!"

"Shh!" Ally hissed at her, trying to cover her mouth before she started chanting loud enough for the whole room to hear.

Cassie licked her hand.

"Eww!" Ally exclaimed, yanking her hand back and wiping it on her jeans. But at the same time, she couldn't help but remember what it used to feel like when Chase kissed her. She wondered if he kissed her now, would it still feel the same way as it did back then?

Distractedly, she took her phone out of her

pocket. "I totally forgot. I need to make some calls back to some people in L.A."

"Sure, you do," Cassie teased her.

"Grams, will you be terribly upset if we cut this visit short and I come back tomorrow to spend more time with you?" Ally asked, ignoring her sister.

"Of course not, dear. It was lovely seeing you again, and I'll see you tomorrow." Her grandmother patted her softly on the arm.

"Hate to break it to you, Grams, but I don't think it's you she's planning to come back to see tomorrow." Ally couldn't resist the childish urge to stick her tongue out at her little sister, who returned the gesture.

"Now Cassie, stop teasing your sister," their grandmother gently chastised her.

"Fine."

"Fine," Ally repeated.

"I'll see you both tomorrow, and I expect you two to be on your best behaviour. You're both grown-ups now. Make sure you behave like it." She gave them both a stern look over the rim of her reading glasses.

"Yes, Grams," they chorused, kissing her on the cheek before heading back out to the car.

Chapter Three

    Chase had always had a particular habit of drumming his fingers against something – his leg, a tabletop, anything – and furrowing his brow while he was thinking. Ally used to tease him and say that it made him look like a serious old man. He was doing this now as he stood in his office, staring out the window at Ally's retreating form.

    Everything and nothing had changed about Ally Hayes in the last six years. Physically, her hair had become a bit lighter, the dark brown now richer with more highlights from all the California sun, but underneath the new look, she was still the same Ally as before. He was glad to see that. She'd reminded him of the good old days, their glorious high school years when they'd felt like they'd run this town. Chase smiled at the memories of him and Ally running through his mind until he was interrupted by a knock on the door behind him.

"Stop looking like a grumpy old man," Fatima teased him.

"I thought, according to you, I *was* a grumpy old man," he teased her back.

"Yeah, but you don't have to act like it. It's not like it was *that* bad seeing Ally again, was it?"

He glanced in her direction, and for a moment, he could see in her dark brown eyes that she was beginning to doubt her earlier conviction.

"No, I suppose it wasn't so bad," he conceded. "And why are you so curious about Ally Hayes, anyways? And why exactly did you invite her to help us out with the dance?" He folded his arms across his chest, giving her a pointed look.

"Well, Kayla was showing me pictures of you, her, Josh, and Ally from when you were kids, and when she showed up here today, I just thought how cool it would be for you two to hang out like you did before. You all seemed so happy then."

Chase softened his look. He couldn't fault her for trying to be the sweet and thoughtful kid she was. He knew she was just trying to cheer him up, given the time of year it was. It was a difficult time for them both. "Well, I suppose that's a good reason."

She smiled at him, glad to see he wasn't mad at her.

"Hey there, you two!" They turned to see Josh Allaby, Chase's best friend and Kayla's fiancé/their current landlord, standing in the doorway.

"Hey! What's up?"

"What are you two looking at? Wait, is that Ally Hayes?" Josh came over to stand next to them, watching the Hayes sisters as they got into their car.

"The one and only."

Yours for the Holiday

"Wow." Josh sat down on the edge of Chase's desk, surprised by this revelation, his lanky frame taking up much of the space beside him.

"Yeah."

"Well, how about that?" Chase could feel him glancing at him sideways, his dark blue eyes full of concern. "So, about dinner tonight," he said, changing the topic. "Kayla sent a text asking if you wanted her to pick up anything while she's at the grocery store?"

Ever since he and Fatima had moved into the granny suite at Josh and Kayla's place, Chase had a standing agreement with them that, as a thank you for keeping their rent so low, he would cook for them once a week. Since he loved to cook, it had really been no bother for him.

"Chase? Did you hear me?"

"What? Oh… Umm…"

"Kayla wanted me to remind you that tonight's your night to cook. She's also about to head to the store, and she wanted to know if you needed her to get anything?" Josh re-read his fiancée's text from his phone.

Chase watched as Ally pulled the car out of the parking lot and drove away. "Uh, yeah, sure. I'll do up a quick list for her." He scribbled a few things on a piece of paper and handed it to him.

Josh nodded. "I'll let her know."

Chase rubbed the palm of his hand across his chin, the stubble making a scratching sound against his palm. "Thanks. Alright, Fatima, I think it's time that we head back to the rec room and start carol practice."

Fatima hopped off her chair and went to the filing cabinet where Chase kept his sheet music. "Ok! Do you think Ally could join us next time?"

"I don't know, kiddo," he replied, trying to put

the thought of Ally from his mind as he ushered her towards the rec room

☙❧

Back at her parents' house, Ally flopped onto her childhood bed. Her bedroom hadn't changed much in the six years since she'd been gone. Her parents had left it much the same as it had been when she'd left after graduation. Her Taylor Swift poster was still fixed to the back of her door, her dark red curtains still hung from the window, lending the room a rosy-coloured hue in the bright winter sun. Her desk in the corner by her closet was still covered in novels she'd read for her senior year English class: *Great Expectations* by Charles Dickens and *Wuthering Heights* by Emily Bronte. Some of her old clothes – whatever wouldn't fit into her suitcase – were still in her closet. She was thankful that she hadn't changed much in size, because she now could use most of her old winter clothes while she was visiting. It was weird being back home; both familiar and yet completely different.

Feeling every hour of the jet lag setting in, she was just considering having a nap before supper when she heard her phone buzz beside her.

"Hello, you," she greeted Liv, opening her video chat.

"Hello, yourself," Liv smiled at her. Ally felt jealous of how radiant Liv looked, make-up free with her hair wrapped up in a colourful headscarf.

"How's Vermont?"

"Take a look for yourself." Liv turned the phone around and gave her a quick tour of the chalet she and Jackson were staying at.

"Wow! Nice place! Jackson's outdone himself. And where is he, by the way?"

"Outside clearing off the deck from the snow we had earlier so we can have a little bonfire later, sit around drinking wine, roasting marshmallows." She turned the phone so Ally could see him.

"Say hi to Ally!" she called out to him, opening the deck door so he could hear her.

"Hi Ally!" he waved to her with a mittened hand.

"Hi Jackson!" she replied, before turning her attention back to Liv. "Snuggling up by a warm fire and watching the snow fall? Well, if that doesn't sound romantic, I don't know what does." Ally propped her chin on her hand.

"It's all just so perfect, isn't it?" Liv replied dreamily.

"Positively Hallmark-esque."

"Where on earth are you?" Liv asked her. "That doesn't look like your apartment."

"I promised you I'd come home for the holidays, so here I am! Welcome to my childhood home." Ally turned her phone around and gave Liv a quick visual tour of her childhood room.

"I thought you told me you weren't going home under *any* circumstances," Liv mocked her.

"Yeah, well, that was before I found out that my Grams had fallen…" her voice trailed off.

"OMG! Is she alright?" Liv's delicate brow furrowed, genuine concern in her dark eyes.

"She's fine," Ally quickly reassured her. "She hurt her hip, and she's got a heart condition that needs monitoring, but overall, she'll be ok. My parents decided they should move her into an old folks' home so that we can all be sure she'll be taken care of, and it's just a few minutes away, so we can see her all the time. In fact, even though I think she'd probably deny it, I think she likes being there. I just got back from visiting her, and she seems to have a lot of company."

"Thank God. I was worried there for a second!"

"Yeah, me too. So, that combined with my run in with Tom right before I left L.A…"

"What?!" Liv's eyes widened in surprise.

"Oh, yeah…" Ally nodded, confirming her worst fears. "So, get this: he has a new girlfriend. A real supermodel-type."

"No!" Liv gasped. "That must've been so intense. What did he say to you? What did you say to him? Tell me everything." She leaned in closer to her phone, rapt with interest.

"We were talking about our Christmas plans, and then she's going on and on about how she was bikini shopping with Tom because, guess what? He's taking her to Hawaii for Christmas."

"No!" Liv gasped again. "*Your* trip to Hawaii? That jerk! How could he do that to you?" Ally had a few choice words that she'd like to call Tom, but "jerk" would suffice for now. "Oh, sweetie! That whole thing must have been horrible. How are you?"

"Surprisingly, I'm ok. You know, I'm beginning to realize now that Tom and I would've never worked out. I mean, if he can replace me that easily, and I couldn't bring myself to be broken up about him when we called it quits, what does that say about our relationship?"

Liv gave her a sympathetic look. "You know what you need now? You need a rebound of your own."

Ally rolled her eyes at her. "Just because I'm over Tom doesn't mean that I'm ready to jump into bed with

Yours for the Holiday

the nearest available guy."

"What is the dating pool like in your town?" Liv interrupted her, ignoring her reluctance. Ally knew her too well; she was definitely not going to let this go so easily. "You know what? You should rebound with the first available guy you've seen since getting home."

"The answer to your first question is: non-existent, and if I were to hook up with the first available guy I've seen since I got home, that would be…"

Chase. The thought momentarily stunned her, rendering her speechless.

"Would be who?" Liv prodded her.

"Uh, that would be my ex-boyfriend, who was getting ready for a dance with my grandmother and a ten-year-old," she responded, gathering herself together.

Liv's eyebrows rose in curiosity.

"Ok, that sounded weirder than it was," Ally admitted. "I meant that there's this Christmas Eve dance being organized at the home where Grams is staying, and apparently, the organizer is none other than my ex-boyfriend and this ten-year-old girl named Fatima."

"Wait, is this *Chase* we're talking about?"

Ally nodded, knowing that she was going to be barraged with a million questions now. She hadn't told Liv much about Chase; just that they'd been high school sweethearts before she'd ended things to pursue her acting dreams. It had all been too painful at the time for her to talk about, and Liv had thankfully not pressed her for the details, but she could tell now that Liv had waited long enough, and she was going to demand some answers.

"Well, go on and tell me more! You've hardly said two words about him in the past. I'm dying to know everything." Her eyes were rapt with attention.

"There's nothing to tell, really…"

"Liar. I know you've been secretly pining over him this whole time. I've seen those little longing stares you give those old high school photos of yours on the walls of your apartment. How was it seeing him again? And what was he doing at the seniors' home? And, more importantly: what did you say to him? What did he say to you? I need *all* the details!"

Ally took a deep breath. "Apparently, he's a music therapist now."

Liv narrowed her eyes. "Didn't you say he was some kind of sports player or something?"

"He was into baseball when we were together. He said he still coaches in his spare time."

She could see Liv making a face that said how cute she thought that was.

"Apparently, he switched career paths in university when his grandmother developed Alzheimer's and he said he wanted to work in music therapy to help improve her memory for as long as he could."

Liv put her hand over her heart. "Oh, my goodness! If that just isn't the sweetest thing I've heard all day. He's good with seniors and kids, and he's very good-looking. I remember that from those photos. I bet he's even hotter now that he's older. He sounds perfect!"

Ally was amazed at how Liv had zeroed in on every single thought she'd had about Chase since she'd seen him this morning. "Um, you *did* hear the part where I told you he was my ex, right?"

"Yeah, but you're single now. Wait, is he single?"

Ally paused for a moment. "I didn't think to ask."

Liv tutted. "Well, did you see a ring on his finger?"

Ally thought back to earlier that day. "I don't

remember one."

"So, who's to say that you couldn't re-ignite some of that old passion between the two of you again?" Liv playfully winked at her.

"The fact that I utterly and unequivocally broke his heart the night of our prom?" Ally suggested.

"Oh, right."

"Yeah. Newsflash: it wasn't pretty."

"Well, I'm sure he's forgotten all about that. It was years ago," Liv said with a dismissive wave of her hand. "I mean, how did he react to seeing you again?"

"I don't know… It was the normal pleasantries, what he's been up to since we last saw each other."

"And?" Liv looked like she was champing at the bit for more information.

"And… That was it, really. He was working, so we didn't have time to really get into anything too deep. Oh, he and Fatima asked me for help in planning the Christmas Eve dance I mentioned earlier."

"Was it his idea or the kid's?" she pressed.

"Chase's."

"Well, that's not nothing!" Liv leaned into the phone a bit more, her interest clearly piqued. "So, who is this kid, anyways?"

"I'm not sure…," Ally admitted. "I didn't think to ask who she belongs to. Maybe she has a grandparent staying there? She did say that the dance was her idea. Or maybe her parents work there, or maybe she was volunteering? I didn't think to ask, but she seemed to know a lot about me." Ally paused a moment to reflect on that.

"Oh, yeah?"

"Yeah, she mentioned how she'd seen some of Chase's old photos of me when I was younger…" Ally now realized how unusual that was.

"Is he…her father?"

"No, couldn't be," Ally replied, surprised by the question. "She was too old to be, unless he'd fathered a kid in high school, and I think I would've remembered that." Still, Ally remembered she'd thought he'd had a fatherly look on his face when Fatima had first joined their conversation. Even though she couldn't be his biological child, there was definitely some kind of deeper connection there that Ally hadn't been told about.

Liv shrugged. "Maybe she's one of the kids he coaches?"

"Could be."

"How you can go through an entire conversation without asking the important questions, I'll never know." Liv shook her head. "You're the worst when it comes to getting gossip."

Ally laughed. "Blame it on the fact that I grew up in a small town where everyone knows everyone else's business. The last thing I want to do now is pry into people's private lives."

Liv rolled her eyes at her. "So, going back to this dance, did he ask just you to help out? Or will this be a group thing?"

"Just me, so I kind of think it'll be the three of us?" She realized she'd forgotten to ask him the details when she'd agreed to help. "We agreed to meet up tomorrow after I visit with Grams for a bit."

"Well!"

"Well, what?" she asked, playing dumb.

"Well, that's your chance, then. To, you know." Liv gave her a you-know-what-I'm-talking-about kind of look.

Ally sighed and rolled over, bringing herself up into a sitting position on the edge of her bed. "I don't

Yours for the Holiday

know…"

"Don't know what?"

"I don't know if that's even what I want," Ally admitted. "I just got out of a relationship, remember? I'm not sure I want to jump back into a new one."

"Who said anything about a relationship?" Liv asked. "You're only there for the holidays, right? Who says you can't just have a little fun under the mistletoe?" Liv gave her a saucy look.

"Liv!"

"Oh, don't be such a prude!" she chastised her. "Have a bit of fun for the holidays. Get back in the game."

"Alright, I'm hanging up now."

Liv playfully stuck her tongue out at her, but didn't tease her any further. "Hey! Before I let you go, have you heard back about that part yet?"

"No, you?" The pit of anxiety in her stomach that she'd been trying to ignore reared its ugly head again.

"No," Liv replied, disappointment in her voice.

"Well, there's still time before it begins filming, so there's still hope," she tried to sound optimistic.

Liv nodded. "If I don't talk to you before Christmas, have a wonderful time!"

"You, too! And, of course, you must tell me the moment anything special happens." Ally winked at her, the two of them knowing she was referencing Liv's potential upcoming engagement.

"And you tell me the moment anything happens on your end." She winked at her.

"Ok, I'm really going now," Ally smiled at her, ending their chat. She was thinking over Liv's advice about Chase when Cassie came by her door.

"Hey, what's the matter?" Cassie paused in the

doorway, a look of concern on her face.

"It's nothing."

"You know, just 'cause you're the big sister, doesn't mean you need to put on a brave face for me." Cassie hopped onto the bed and settled down on the pillow beside her, the two of them looking up at the ceiling. Ally glanced over at her younger sister and smiled. They both knew that, even though Cassie was the younger one, she'd always been the braver one. Ally had always admired how her sister had always been so confident, always so perfectly content with being who she was, unlike Ally, who'd always felt like she'd been trying to live up to everyone's expectations, not least of all, her own.

"It's just… well, things in L.A. might not be going as well as I've led you, Mom, and Dad to believe," she admitted. It felt good to finally say it out loud. She'd always felt a little hesitant, a little ashamed of admitting to her family that her "perfect" Los Angeles life wasn't nearly as perfect as they thought.

"Can I tell you something?" Cassie asked.

"Yeah."

"I know," Cassie admitted.

"You do?" Ally turned and propped her head up on her hand. The revelation shocked her.

"Yeah. I've kind of suspected for awhile now, actually."

"Wait… what? How?"

Cassie chuckled. "You're not as good at your poker face as you think you are."

Ally settled onto her back again, staring up at the white ceiling above them. "Huh. Why didn't you say anything?"

"I figured you'd tell me when you were ready," Cassie shrugged. "I figured you just needed some time."

Yours for the Holiday

Ally nodded.

"So, what's really going on in L.A.?" This time, Cassie was the one who turned over to look at her sister.

"Well, it's *hard*," Ally admitted. "So much harder than I thought it would be. I mean, of course it's going to be hard: I'm a nobody from a place no one's even heard of."

"You're not a nobody!" Cassie lightly smacked her arm.

"Well, I am in L.A." Her face took on a forlorn expression for a moment. "I have to work part-time at this café down the street from where I live in order to make the rent, for one. And I live in this tiny apartment, for another. And all I seem to do is go to auditions and get judged by people who only see me for a few minutes out of the day and know nothing about me or seem to care how hard I prepared for that audition because they don't like the fact that my hair colour happened to be the wrong shade from what they were looking for that day."

"Everyone in L.A. starts out as a server, don't they?" Cassie asked, as if this was nothing unusual.

"Yeah, but…"

"You just thought it'd be different for you because you're special?" Her sister gave her a know-it-all look.

"Well, when you put it that way, it sounds silly."

"I don't think it's silly." Cassie's tone was serious. "I just think you had an unrealistic vision in your head of what it would take to succeed there, or how long it would take. Look, everyone's on their own journey and you can't compare yourself to the others. Your big break *will* come."

"How can you be so sure?" she asked, seriously. "I mean, how long do I keep trying before I give up and realize that it's not what I'm meant to do?"

"Let me ask you this: after all the auditions and people judging you on your looks or the sound of your voice, and comparing you to the hundreds of other women going for that same audition, do you still love acting?"

"Yes," Ally replied without hesitation.

"Then there you go," Cassie shrugged as if it was a no-brainer.

"So, you're saying I shouldn't give up on acting?"

"I'm saying that you should keep going until you get your big break, because if you don't, I'm seriously going to punch you." A big smile broke out on her sister's face.

Ally chuckled.

"I'm serious! This is what you've wanted to do your whole life. You don't give up on it just because things are tough right now. You keep fighting for it, because all the best things are worth fighting for."

"Thanks for the pep talk, sis." She reached out and squeezed her sister's hand.

"Any time."

The two of them lay there for a moment, just staring at the ceiling when Cassie spoke. "So, the reason I came up here is because Mom needs some help with the groceries. C'mon, you're coming with me to get them."

"Fine," she groaned melodramatically, getting up and following her little sister down the stairs. She hurriedly put on her boots, trying to keep up with Cassie, who was out the door and in the car before Ally could button her coat.

"C'mon, slowpoke!" Cassie called from the car as Ally pulled the front door closed behind her.

"I'm coming, I'm coming," she grumbled, getting

Yours for the Holiday

into the car, the two of them heading off to the store. Forty minutes later, the two of them were walking around the store, checking the list their mother had given them.

"Bread?"

"Check," Cassie confirmed, ticking it off.

"Cranberries?"

"Check."

"Spices for the stuffing... We got those," Cassie crossed those off the list as well, after peering into the cart. Ally picked them up and gave them a sniff to make sure that Cassie had picked up fresh ones.

"Eggnog?"

"Mmm... nope. We still need to get some."

"And what about flour?"

"Nope, still need to get some of that, too."

"Alright, let's divide and conquer. You get the flour, and I'll get the eggnog," Ally told her sister as she steered the shopping cart toward the dairy aisle.

The store was busy, which wasn't really all that surprising given the time of year. People were out getting stocked up on all their essentials for the holidays, even though the grocery store would only be closed on Christmas Day. However, Maritimers had always been the type of people who liked to come prepared for anything, so that meant having an over-stocked pantry for those last-minute, unexpected guests that might arrive for Christmas dinner. Christmas music played over the grocery store's PA system, and Ally hummed along to Amy Grant's "Rockin' Around the Christmas Tree." Just as she'd reached the section of the aisle with the eggnog, she heard a voice behind her.

"Ally? OMG! Is that really you?" She turned around, recognizing the familiar voice.

"Kayla?!" Abandoning her cart where it stood,

Ally rushed towards her best friend from high school.

"It's so good to see you!" Kayla pulled her into a hug.

"It's so good to see you, too! God, it's been…" She paused when she realized she hadn't seen or spoken to her in six years. She and Kayla had once been as close as sisters, but not only had she never called Kayla since moving to Los Angeles, she'd barely emailed or remembered to send a Christmas card. She'd just been one of the many casualties after her break-up with Chase. An enormous wave of guilt washed over her.

"Well, it's great that you're back now," Kayla said cheerily, trying to cover up the awkward pause. "You're back to see your Grams, I bet."

"Yeah. Did Mom and Dad tell you she'd fallen down and hurt herself?"

"Yeah. I mean, no, Josh had told me she was being moved into the nursing home the other week."

Ally raised an inquisitive brow, wondering how Josh would've known about her grandmother moving into the home. "Did he hear that from Chase?"

"No… wait, have you seen Chase since you've been back?" Kayla seemed to be both surprised and apprehensive about this revelation. There was something almost protective about the way she asked it, but who she was protecting – Ally or Chase – she couldn't say exactly. She couldn't blame her; Ally had left a wave of destruction in her wake when she'd left town, and Chase, Kayla, and Josh had all been swept up in it. The four of them had once been the closest of friends since childhood; now she felt like they'd almost become strangers to her.

"Yeah, I saw him earlier today at the nursing home when I was visiting with Grams."

Kayla seemed surprised. "Wow, that's… great."

Yours for the Holiday

Ally couldn't help but notice the way she paused.

"Josh and Chase didn't mention anything about seeing you earlier."

Ally must've had another look of confusion on her face, for Kayla said, "Sorry, Josh is actually the manager at the nursing home where your Grams lives. He and Chase work there together."

It was Ally's turn to be surprised.

"Yeah, who would've thought those two would've become responsible grown ups, eh?" Kayla teased, noticing her expression. "Certainly not me. I thought I was going to be married to a hockey player. It totally floored me when Josh switched into business, and then even more so when he was made the manager of the nursing home. Not that I'm complaining. It's much safer and more sensible than hockey."

"How'd that come about?" Ally asked.

"Well, Chase had become the music therapist there, and not long after, the old manager had retired. So, Chase put in a good word for Josh, and the rest is history."

"I feel awful for not calling as much as I should have," she admitted, feeling guilty that she had missed out on all this news.

"Well, I could've called, too," Kayla replied, putting a gentle hand on her forearm. "I could use the wedding planning as an excuse, but the truth is, I'm just bad at keeping in touch."

"Wedding planning?" Ally asked, reflexively looking down at her hand and noticing the small diamond ring. "Wait, don't tell me that Josh Allaby finally proposed to you?"

Everyone had known since they were kids that Josh and Kayla would get married one day. Of course, they'd said the same thing about her and Chase, too, but she'd had no doubts that Josh and Kayla were definitely endgame.

Kayla held up her hand so Ally could see the small diamond with its simple setting. She suddenly felt the enormity of her friend's momentous, life-changing event. It made Ally feel like everything she'd done up to that point had just been her playing at being a grown up, while all along, her friends were the ones who were the real grown-ups. She was a little sad, too. There was once a time when she and Kayla had told each other literally everything about their lives. Now, she'd gone and missed one of the most important announcements in her friend's life because she hadn't been here when it had happened.

"Congratulations!" Ally gave her a slightly watery smile.

"Thanks! Hey, what are you doing tonight?" Kayla asked, perhaps noticing Ally's expression.

"Um… I don't know…" Ally said, looking to Cassie, who'd found the flour and returned to find her sister. Cassie shrugged and went back to looking at her phone.

"Great, it's settled. You're coming over to our place for supper. We can all get caught up on the last few years, and I'm sure Fatima would be thrilled to have you over, too." Kayla's enthusiasm made it so that Ally felt like she couldn't refuse.

"Alright then." She smiled at her. "Well, we should finish up the rest of this shopping before Mom wonders where we are." Ally gestured to the half-full cart in front of her and the shopping list in her hand.

"Yeah, of course. Me too." Kayla gestured to her own cart. "And I should find my fiancé. I left him wandering around the snack aisle, which is never a good thing."

"Great, so what time should I be at your place?" she asked.

"I'll text you the details later," Kayla promised.

"Great, here's my number." Ally took Kayla's phone and put her number in her contact list. "See you tonight!"

"See you then!"

༄༅

"There you are!" Kayla caught up with her fiancé. His arms were full of chip bags. She gave him a pointed look as he sheepishly returned one of the bags. This continued until Josh only had one bag left in his hands.

"Fine," he groaned, putting his remaining bag of chips in the cart.

"Much better," Kayla replied, pleased. "You don't need all those snacks anyways. We have plenty of munchies at home already."

Josh threw her a glance that stated that he did not agree with this assessment. Kayla chose to ignore him.

"You'll never guess who I just ran into," she said, changing the topic.

"It wouldn't happen to have been Ally Hayes, would it?" he asked casually.

"Why didn't you tell me she was in town?" Kayla punched him lightly on the arm.

"Ow!"

"Oh, I barely touched you," she snapped back.

He rubbed his arm, nevertheless. "I completely forgot. I'm sorry." He reached over to pull her into his arms for a kiss, and she reluctantly acquiesced.

"I suppose I forgive you." Josh smiled happily at her. "Oh, and Ally's going to be joining us for dinner tonight, by the way."

Josh paused a moment. "Ally's going to be joining us tonight?" he repeated. "Isn't tonight Chase's night to cook?" he asked, picking up a head of lettuce as they moved into the vegetable aisle and placed it in the shopping cart. "Oh... *oh*!" he said, the pieces of his fiancée's plan all clicking into place. "Oh no. No, no, no."

"Oh yes," Kayla counter-argued, picking up some carrots and celery and placing them in the cart beside the lettuce.

"Oh no. I'm not going to be a part of some plan to 'accidentally' get Chase and Ally together. No way. That ship sailed a long time ago. They've both moved on." Josh shook his head emphatically.

"Well, I didn't see a ring on her finger, and you and I both know he hasn't dated anyone since Samar. Chase needs to get back out there again." She gave him a smug look, daring him to disagree with her.

"You're playing with fire," he warned her. "You know how things ended between the two of them. I'm sorry, but after seeing what he went through the first time with Ally, then with Samar, I just can't watch him get his heart broken like that again. Are you really so quick to make him go through all that again?"

Josh gave her a serious look this time.

"Of course, I don't want to see him hurt, but he's hurting now by not living. And then there's Fatima to think about."

"Exactly." Josh pointed at her, emphasizing his argument. "Do you really think Ally's the kind of person who's going to put aside her acting dreams to become the kind of role model she needs?"

Yours for the Holiday

"Well, we'll never know unless we put them together," Kayla replied. "I just want him to be as happy as we are."

Josh came up to her and put his hands on either side of her shoulders. "I know you do, and I know that Ally's been one of our best friends since childhood and it's easy to get swept up in all that charm of hers, but just remember, it's not just his heart we have to look out for. There's a little girl who we don't want to end up brokenhearted, too."

"Still, don't you think it would be great if… you know…?"

"No, I don't know, and I don't want to know," Josh said firmly, trying to put an end to the conversation.

"All I'm saying is that Chase and Ally haven't seen each other in years. Who knows what could happen if the two of them have a nice dinner together?"

"For future reference, when this all blows up in your face, I'm totally blaming it all on you." Josh picked up some boxes of cereal from the shelf and put them in the cart as they continued throughout the store.

"Well, we'll see about that." Kayla gave him a cheery but determined smile as she pushed their cart towards the checkout.

Chapter Four

    Later that night, Ally drove the short distance outside the city limits to the small village of Penniac, where Josh and Kayla now lived. The forest-lined roads were lit only by the moon and her headlights reflecting off the snow. As she made her way up the long lane to the circular driveway in front of the house, she gazed up at the beautiful farmhouse in front of her. She parked by the garage, noticing the place had come complete with a barn for the horses that Kayla had said she'd always wanted, as well as a granny suite at the back of the house. The white icicle lights decorating the wrap-around porch cast a cozy glow in the dark night. It was the perfect mood-setter for the holiday season. Stepping onto the front porch, Ally rang the bell, hearing the old chiming tune ring throughout the big house.

    "Hi, Ally! Come in, come in!" Kayla welcomed

Yours for the Holiday

her, opening up the screen door for her. She was smartly dressed in a red cashmere sweater and a nice pair of slacks. "Let me take your coat for you."

"Thanks!" Ally relinquished her winter coat to her, smoothing down her black and gold short-sleeved shirt with a bowtie neck. She was glad that she'd dressed up a bit for the occasion.

"You have a gorgeous place here." Josh and Kayla had decorated their home in a variety of warm hues accentuated by the earthy tones of the furniture, giving the place a lived-in, country home feel.

"Thanks! Would you like a tour?"

"Can I show her?" Fatima asked, scampering down the hallway.

Ally was surprised, and a little confused, to see her. "Hi Fatima! I didn't know you'd be here tonight."

"Chase and I live here," the young girl replied, as if this was obvious to everyone.

"You do?" Ally had a stunned look on her face.

"Yeah. Come on! I'll show you around!" Fatima reached out and took her hand, pulling Ally down the hallway to begin the tour, as Kayla gave her an I'll-tell-you-later look.

"Ok, then," Ally said, letting herself be led through the house. Fatima took her through all the rooms on the ground floor, proudly showing off each one.

"And this hallway connects to our part of the house," Fatima said, gesturing to the granny suite.

"Your part of the house?" Ally repeated, still wondering what connection the girl had to Josh, Kayla, and Chase, for that matter.

"Come on. I'll show you." She led her down the hallway to a door that opened up into a small, two-storey apartment at the back of the house. She stood in the open-concept kitchen/living room, decorated in shades of black and white. The place definitely had a masculine feel, except for the brightly coloured rugs and decorative throws enhancing the living room. Ally felt like she was intruding into Chase's private space, but still had the urge to search the room for insights into the person he'd become in the time since she'd been away. However, she was distracted by Fatima.

"Come on! I want to show you my room." She bounded up the stairs to the second floor, gesturing for Ally to follow. As she followed her up the staircase, she noticed a series of black-and-white photographs of Chase, Fatima, and a beautiful woman she'd never seen before, but who distinctly looked like a relative of Fatima's. The photos appeared to have been taken over the span of a few years: one of them featured the woman holding a baby that Ally assumed was Fatima, another showed the three of them playing outside in the leaves on a sunny autumn day; another showed Chase embracing the mystery woman.

"Are you coming?" Fatima asked, interrupting her snooping.

"Yeah, of course." Ally cleared her throat and headed up the remaining stairs, pondering this new piece of the puzzle into Chase's life.

"Wow! This is some room!" she exclaimed, stepping inside the purple-painted room. It had a distinctly feminine feel, completely different from the functionality of the kitchen and living room area.

"You like it?"

"I like it," she replied, nodding her approval. "Did you put all these stars up by yourself?" she asked, pointing to the ceiling where a bunch of glow-in-the-dark stars had been placed.

Yours for the Holiday

"No," Fatima giggled. "Mummy put them up for me. She used to say to me that it didn't matter where in the world we were, the stars would always shine for me."

Ally thought she felt her heart melt a little. She glanced around the room. There was an interesting mix of posters of both cute animals and pop stars, as well as more photos of her with the mystery woman, whom Ally now assumed was Fatima's mother, and Chase.

"Well, she sounds like a very special mom, indeed."

"Yeah. I miss her." Fatima's face clouded over a bit and Ally felt a wave of compassion come over her. Even though she'd only just met her this morning, she was beginning to feel a connection with this girl she'd only just met this morning.

"She died a few years ago," Fatima explained, picking up one of the photographs of her mother from her bedside table and gazing lovingly at it. Ally's face contorted into an expression of sadness. It was sad knowing that someone so young had lost someone so close to them.

"I'm so sorry, Fatima." What else was there she could say?

"But I still have Chase." A little of the sadness left her voice as Fatima smiled at a photo of her and Chase at what looked like the Hopewell Rocks.

"He's pretty awesome, isn't he?" Ally asked, realizing her connection to Chase: he was her parent. Maybe not biologically, but he was certainly a parental figure to her, nonetheless.

"Yeah, he is." A big smile returned to Fatima's face.

"Hey, we should probably get back. Kayla's going to think we got lost," she said, trying to inject a bit of

59

enthusiasm back into her voice. The two of them headed back through the granny suite to the main house.

"Ally?" a familiar voice called out as they walked down the hallway to the living room.

"Josh? Hey there, stranger." She reached out and gave him a big hug. "It's good to see you again."

"It's good to see you, too." She was glad to hear him say this. After the way she'd left, she wasn't sure if Josh would want to see her again. Even though the four of them had once been so close, Josh had always been Chase's best friend. She knew she couldn't have put him in an easy position when she'd left, having to clean up her mess.

"Was Fatima showing you around the place?"

"Yeah, she was being quite the tour guide. You have a lovely home here."

"Thanks. It still needs a bit of work in some spots, but that's the joy of owning a home, right?" Ally nodded politely. She'd never owned her own place before, and with the way her career was going, she wondered if she ever would.

"Would you two like some eggnog?" Kayla asked, appearing with a drink tray.

"Sure, that sounds great," Ally replied, making herself comfortable on the dark green chesterfield by the fire, letting it warm her chilly bones. Josh and Kayla's place was just as expertly decorated inside as it was outside. A miniature porcelain village decorated the fireplace mantle. Their tree glittered with white and gold decorations, taking up one whole corner of the room. The scent of fresh pine needles mingled with the scent of the burning logs and whatever was cooking in the kitchen. The coziness of it all filled Ally with a sense of warmth and happiness. These were the things she'd missed about

Yours for the Holiday

living in Los Angeles: the smell of cold in the dead of winter, the cheer that came with being around old friends, the scent of good, home-cooked meals from the kitchen. Sure, back in Los Angeles she had Liv, whom she wouldn't trade for the world, but somehow, it just wasn't the same. Being back home was like a balm for her weary soul.

"Ok, here we go." Kayla placed a drinks tray on the coffee table and handed the drinks to them. "This one's for you, and this one's for you."

She gave each one a quick sniff before handing them over.

"I put a little something in yours that's just for the adults," she whispered to Ally, giving her a wink. Ally took a small sip and detected a hint of rum and nutmeg mixed in with the thick eggnog.

"So, the famous actress returns!" Josh said, after a moment, settling himself onto a nearby chair.

Ally blushed. "I'm hardly a famous actress."

"Oh, come now. We all saw that modelling campaign you did," Kayla said, sitting down next to her on the chesterfield. "Your Grams was showing that magazine around to everyone she talked to, telling them about her famous granddaughter."

Ally smiled at the thought of how proud her grandmother was of her. It was just what she'd needed to hear. The constant cycle of auditions and rejections could all be a bit soul-crushing. It was nice hearing that someone still believed in her, even if she doubted herself sometimes.

"Well, enough about me. What about you two? You have this house, you got engaged. Soon enough, you'll be married with kids running around this place. It's like you went from high school graduates to full-blown grown ups in what feels like point two seconds." Seeing them here in their house made Ally feel much younger than Josh and Kayla, even though they were the same age. They had their lives together, and here she was with just a tiny, generic apartment and unstable job prospects. She was hardly making her mark upon the world compared to the friends.

"You don't want to hear about us; we're boring! We're just an ordinary elementary teacher and a nursing home manager trying to make enough money to pay the bills. You, on the other hand. You're the one who has this whole fancy life in L.A."

"Of course, I want to hear about that! You two are doing amazing work sculpting the minds of the future and taking care of our seniors. It's exactly the kind of news I want to catch up on. And one modelling gig is hardly a career," Ally was quick to point out. Even though she'd been the face of one of the biggest make-up brands in North America in a short-lived ad campaign, she'd still spent most of her days sitting by the phone waiting for her agent to call her with more gigs. It had been months of auditions for bit parts that never panned out before her agent finally called with the supporting role in the upcoming rom-com she and Liv had auditioned for just before she got here.

"Come on! Tell me all about living in L.A. Have you met Ryan Gosling yet? Or one of the Hemsworth brothers? Ah! I'm sure you run into celebrities all the time."

"Yeah, sure. All the time," she replied sarcastically. "No, really, my life is all about auditions and acting classes, and waiting to hear back from casting agents, only to find out I'm not right for the part. It's really not as glamourous as what you've got pictured in your head. I've

Yours for the Holiday

been to three nightclubs the whole time I've lived there, and never once saw a celebrity. I watch the Oscars the same way everyone else does: on the TV at home, sitting on the couch with a tub of ice cream and a bowl of popcorn. Honestly, my life's kind of no different than if I'd just stayed here and gone to university like the rest of you." At least then she would've been a part of big events like Josh and Kayla's engagement.

"Oh, it can't be all that bad," Kayla reassured her.

"Hey, what's for supper?" Ally asked, changing the topic. A delectable scent wafted in from the kitchen.

"I don't know exactly… I forgot to ask Chase, but whatever it is, it smells great, doesn't it?" Kayla replied.

Ally nearly spluttered her drink. "Chase is cooking for us?"

She supposed she should've expected this, given that he apparently lived here, a fact that Kayla had conveniently left out when she'd extended the invitation for supper. But still, the mention of his name, especially after finding out he'd had this whole other life while she was gone, was enough to cause her a little anxiety.

"Yeah, it's his night to cook," Josh confirmed, exchanging a glance with Kayla. "We give him a bit of a discount on rent if he cooks for us once or twice a week. And you know him; he loves to cook for people."

She did know. Chase had always been an excellent cook. Ever since they were kids, she'd told him that if his baseball career didn't work out, he should become a chef and open his own restaurant, which had made his switch into music therapy even more surprising to her. When she'd decided to move to Los Angeles, she'd even tried to convince him to come with her and go to culinary school, but he'd taken the safer route by staying home and going to university instead.

"Well, supper's just about to be served," Chase announced, coming through the passageway from the kitchen, as if talking about him had made him appear. "Oh, hi Ally. I didn't know you were coming over tonight."

Ally noted that his tone didn't sound entirely disappointed, and she felt a bit of a thrill running down her spine. It was astonishing how, after all this time, he could still make her feel like she was a girl with a crush again every time she was around.

"I met Ally in the grocery store earlier and I invited her. We can't have her be in town and not have her over."

"I hope that's ok?" Ally gave him an apologetic look.

"Yeah, of course." He smiled at her in response. Ally couldn't help but notice the smug look Kayla threw Josh, and she knew without a doubt that there was nothing unplanned about this little run-in at all.

"Well, should we move into the dining room?" Kayla asked, gesturing to everyone in the room, likely before anyone started accusing her of trying to set Chase and Ally. They rose from their seats and followed her down the hallway to the dining room.

"This is gorgeous!" Ally was continuously surprised at how talented Kayla was with decorating. "Seriously, it looks like it could be featured in a magazine. Have you considered quitting your day job and staging homes? Or becoming a home decorator? I'd pay you good money to transform my apartment in L.A. into something gorgeous like this."

"I can't say that I wouldn't be excited to do a job like that, but I'd miss the little rugrats too much, even if they do drive me up the wall with their questions every day," she said mirthfully as they sat down at the table.

"Here we go." Chase entered the room carrying a tray in his oven-mittened hands.

"That smells divine." Ally breathed in the scent, her stomach grumbling at the thought of dinner to come.

"What is it?" Fatima asked, looking at it curiously.

"Coq au vin, scalloped potatoes, and root vegetables seasoned with rosemary." Ally felt her mouth watering.

"Bon appétit." Chase gestured for them to begin eating.

"Dude, I think you've outdone yourself," Josh said around a forkful of chicken. "This is definitely the best thing you've ever made for us." He quickly shoveled another mouthful in after the first.

"Slow down and leave some for the rest of us," Kayla teased him.

"I completely agree with Josh." Ally closed her eyes, a small smile forming on her lips.

Chase smiled at her, one of those rare, genuine smiles he used to save just for her. She felt butterflies in her stomach and her cheeks growing red as she gazed into those dark eyes of his. She was suddenly aware of how close she was sitting to him, how she could smell his aftershave, how their elbows nearly bumped into each other each time they took a forkful of food, causing a little thrill to run through her each time. Perhaps realizing that his gaze had lingered longer than he'd intended, he cleared his throat and turned his attention back to his plate.

"Would anyone like a freshly baked roll?" Kayla asked, smiling at the both of them, clearly pleased with the fruits of her plan to put them together. "Chase made them this afternoon."

Ally reached over and grabbed two from the top of the basket. "I hope these are your grandmother's recipe?"

"Of course," Chase confirmed, seemingly pleased that she recognized the recipe.

"I wouldn't think that actresses would be allowed to eat bread," Josh stated, observing Ally as she slathered butter onto her rolls. He hadn't meant it to be rude, but still, Kayla elbowed him in the side.

"What? I just thought that actors were all concerned about their weight," Josh replied, his tone demonstrating that he didn't know what he'd said wrong.

"Actually, L.A.'s all about body-positivity now," Ally said, letting him off the hook. "I mean, don't get me wrong; there's still plenty of directors and casting directors who are way too focused on still judging women by their size, but there have been calls for Hollywood to diversify more. Besides, I feel like given the exercise routine Liv's going to have me doing in the new year, I have a right to eat whatever I like over Christmas."

"Oh? And who's this Liv person?" Kayla asked, latching onto any news of Ally's life in Los Angeles.

"A friend I met out in L.A. the first week I arrived," Ally replied, loading up her fork with more food. "She's an actress, just like me. She's been such a godsend; I don't know what I'd have done that first week without her, or ever since then, really. I probably would've gotten on the next plane right back here to Fredericton if she hadn't talked me off the ledge a number of times."

"Sounds like we should be cursing her instead of praising her, then, for keeping you out there so long," Chase replied. The comment completely took her, and everyone, by surprise. "I just mean, it wouldn't have been all that bad had you come home that summer instead of staying out there," he said, quickly. Ally realized, then, that perhaps that had been what he'd been hoping for all along: that she would come back home, come back to him.

"Have you got a boyfriend in L.A.?" Fatima asked in that way that only young children can get away with, interrupting her thoughts. "Chase isn't dating anyone, by the way."

Ally nearly choked on her bite of her chicken and noticed that Chase had nearly done the same.

"No, no boyfriend," she confirmed, carefully swallowing, trying not to laugh. "I was dating someone for a few years, but we recently broke up."

A look came over Chase's face, a mixture of emotions she couldn't quite read. There was a time she could read every single one of his expressions, but now, after so long away, it was like re-learning a language she'd almost forgotten.

"Why'd you two break up?" Fatima asked.

"Fatima! What have I told you about prying into people's personal lives?" Chase gave her an apologetic look. "I'm sorry. She's just really direct, sometimes."

Ally gave him a look that said that she didn't think that Fatima had dug this particular trait out of the ground, especially given his confession only moments before that he'd secretly hoped all this time that she'd come home earlier.

"It's fine." Ally waved a hand dismissively. "We just wanted different things, in the end. We're both actors, and you know what they say if you're an actor: you don't date other actors. We make the worst partners because we're never in the same place for very long. It's tough to make a relationship work when one person is hardly ever around."

This time it was her turn to look sorry, sorry for putting her dreams ahead of him, sorry for leaving him behind the way she did, sorry for staying away so long. It hadn't been an easy decision for her, leaving him like that. She desperately hoped he knew that, that he didn't think she'd just left him without a second thought.

"Well, I think it's good you two broke up," Fatima replied, surprising her.

"Fatima!" Chase exclaimed once more.

"I just meant that it's good she's not with someone who isn't meant for her!" the young girl replied defensively.

"Still, I think you should apologize."

"Sorry," Fatima mumbled, pushing some of the vegetables around her plate.

"That's ok," Ally reassured her. "You're right. In the end, we weren't meant to be, and it probably is for the best."

Fatima shot Chase a told-you-so look, but wisely chose not to gloat about it.

"So, how are the three of you getting on with planning the dance?" Josh asked, safely steering the conversation in a more neutral direction.

"Well, they did only ask me to help this morning, so it's not like we've had much time to talk about it," Ally admitted.

"But I'm confident now that Ally's onboard that it's going to be spectacular," Chase supplied. Ally gave him a warm smile. "Do you guys remember those epic parties Ally used to have in high school?"

"Yes!" Kayla's entire face lit up. "Remember that Hallowe'en party you had, Al, and Chester got himself all covered in Cassie's container of glow-in-the-dark glitter she had?"

Yours for the Holiday

"Poor Chester," Ally reminisced about the Hayes family's deceased golden retriever. "He was still luminescent for months afterwards."

"He loved it," Josh chuckled as he thought back to that night. "I remember Chase and I having to run around trying to catch him so we could take him to the vet to make sure he didn't ingest any of the stuff. I swear that dog was laughing at the two of us as we chased him around the house, trying to get hold of him."

The four of them laughed mirthfully, recounting plenty of their epic high school memories to Fatima. It made Ally relax, reminding her of old times when the four of them were happier, when they didn't feel so awkward around one another.

"Anyone up for dessert?" Chase asked as the evening drew to a close.

Josh and Kayla both shook their heads politely. "I don't think I could eat another bite."

"Oh, come on, now. There's a wonderful mincemeat pie in there."

Ally shook her head when he glanced her way. "None for me, thanks." She knew it was a Christmas tradition, but she'd never favoured mincemeat. "Actually, I think I'm going to head out. You, me, and Fatima have a long day tomorrow, it seems."

Josh and Kayla gently protested the idea of her leaving so early, but they didn't press her.

"I'll see you tomorrow, then," she smiled at Chase and Fatima.

"Actually, would you mind giving me a ride back to my parents' place?" he asked, surprising her. "My dad asked if I'd take a look at his truck for him and I thought, since you're going in that direction anyways, that I might hitch a ride with you. Josh, Kayla, do you mind looking after Fatima for me tonight?"

"Yeah, sure. No problem. Josh, Kayla, thank you for dinner." She gave them both a quick hug.

"Love you, kiddo," Chase said to Fatima, giving her a hug. "Be good for Josh and Kayla, alright? I'll be back later when I take a look at Pepère's truck."

"Ok," Fatima muffled into his coat.

Ally buttoned up her coat and followed Chase out into the chilly night. "Brrr... it's so cold out!" Ally blew on her exposed fingers.

"Where are your mitts?"

"Uh, I'm lucky that my parents still had one of my old winter coats from high school lying around, otherwise I wouldn't even have this." She pointed at her black peacoat. "It's not exactly like it gets below zero in California. And, apparently, when I was in high school, I thought I was too cool for mittens, because there weren't any left in my pockets when I went to put them on earlier. That, or Cassie borrowed them and never gave put them back."

"Yeah, Josh and I never understood how you and Kayla could wear skirts and bare legs in the middle of winter," Chase reminisced about their high school days. "It's amazing how you two didn't freeze to death before graduation."

"Ah, the joys of being young and stupid, and thinking it's cool to freeze your butt off," Ally laughed, blowing onto her fingers once more.

"Here, take this, and this." He took off his scarf and wrapped it around her neck, tucking up under her chin and trying to cover her ears with it.

"I feel like the abominable snowman," she complained.

"I think you look beautiful," Chase said, his voice soft. "You always looked pretty with snow falling all around you. Makes your eyes twinkle."

Her cheeks flushed red, and it wasn't only from the cold.

"Here." Chase handed her one of his mittens.

"What about you? Aren't you going to freeze?"

"We're only going to your car. It's not like I'm going to lose a finger between here and there," he chuckled. "Put this one on, and I'll put mine on and stick my other hand in my pocket," he said, showing her. "Now, you put your other hand here." He gestured to the crook of his arm. She hesitated for half a second, but the prospect of having some of the feeling in her fingers again was too much to resist. She tucked her hand in the crook of his right elbow, and he brought it in close to his body.

"There," he said with a satisfied tone. "Now, that'll get us to the car and then we can get the heat on."

"Lead the way." When they got inside the car, she turned the heater up full blast, freezing cold air hitting them right in the face.

"Another great thing about L.A. is that I don't have to get into a frozen car every day," she complained, turning the fans down, and waiting for her car engine to warm up.

"Yeah, L.A. sounds great, even if you tried to make it sound otherwise earlier."

She gave him a curious look.

"I overheard you talking to Josh and Kayla earlier," Chase admitted.

"Why didn't you come out sooner and join in on the conversation, then?" she asked, putting the car in drive.

"The truth is, I was too shy to come out and see you."

"Chase Cormier, shy?" she teased. She could

think of a lot of adjectives to describe Chase, but shy wasn't one of them.

"Yeah, well, intimidated might be a better word?" His voice sounded serious now.

"Intimidated by me?" She was genuinely astounded by this news. She never would've described herself as intimidating.

"Not intimidated by you, per se, but just that you seem to have it all together. Most of the time, I feel like I'm just trying to make it through the day." There was an uncharacteristic sadness to his voice now, and it pained her to hear it. After all this time, the thought that something had hurt him while she'd been away hurt her, too. "In university, I kind of felt like I was drifting through it all until my grandmother got her Alzheimer's. It was only then that I settled on music therapy. I just wonder sometimes how you could be so sure of what you wanted to do back in high school, and how you could stick with it all this time."

"Do you love it?" Ally asked. She could tell by the way he shifted in his seat that the question had taken off-guard.

"Yeah, I do, actually. Working at the nursing home turned out to be one of the best decisions of my life."

She felt happy for him. She hadn't known what to think of seeing him again after all these years, let alone how she'd still feel about him, but she only wanted to see him happy. That was all she'd ever wanted for him.

"Then at least you're one up on me."

She could feel Chase's eyes on her in the dark interior of the car, like they were boring a hole into her soul.

"What do you mean?"

Yours for the Holiday

"Despite what you may have thought you overheard tonight, my life is far from perfect. The truth is, before Mom called to tell me about Grams, I was wondering if I should move back home for good." She let that information sink in. Chase was silent, but she could tell he was mulling the words over, waiting for her to finish. He'd always been good like that, knowing exactly when to just let her talk until she was done.

"I just didn't want to come home and seem like an enormous failure, you know? I mean, I still love acting. I know it's what I want to do, it's just that maybe I aimed too high, too soon. Maybe I'm just meant to be a community theatre actress and not a Hollywood actress."

"I don't believe that for a second, and neither do you."

It filled her with an indescribable kind of happiness to hear that from him.

"Look, to set the record straight, when you left, it wasn't that I wasn't being supportive of your dreams. I just didn't think moving out to L.A. right after high school was the right decision for you, at the time. And yeah, a part of me was being a selfish teenager who wanted his girlfriend to stay with him, but I've always known you were made to be on the big screen. After a couple of years to think things over, I think it was good that you left; this place is too small for you."

She was sad to hear that he couldn't seem to picture her living here again, because that meant that he saw no hope for the two of them. She wasn't sure why that made her sad; it wasn't like she'd come here with the intention of getting back together with him, and yet, she would have been lying if she'd said that the thought hadn't briefly crossed her mind.

The two of them fell quiet as she processed this

information, and they finished the rest of the journey in silence. All too soon, she pulled into her parents' driveway and turned off the car.

"Ally?"

"Yeah?"

He shifted in his seat to look at her, his face dimly lit from the streetlights, the snow softly falling around them. "Do me a favour?"

"Yeah, sure."

"Give L.A. another shot. I have a feeling your big break will come soon, and you'd only regret it if you gave up on your dream now."

"I promise," she said, not knowing what else to say. For him, she'd still do just about anything. Maybe being home and seeing him again was dredging up some old feelings, but Ally felt herself leaning towards him. As she drew closer, Chase cleared his throat, stopping her in her tracks.

"So, we'll see you tomorrow?"

"Right," she said, remembering how Fatima had brought them together to plan the dance. "We could go to Joe's, like we used to?"

"Yeah, we could do that," he nodded, then pointed toward his parents' place. "I should, uh, head inside."

"Yeah, me too." She followed him outside, the blast of cold air sending a shiver down her spine. "Well, I'll see you tomorrow, I guess."

"Goodnight, Al."

She quietly climbed the front steps and headed inside, closing the door behind her and leaned against it. "Great job, Ally. Great job."

She didn't think things could get any more awkward between her and Chase, but then she'd only gone

Yours for the Holiday

ahead and nearly tried to kiss him, and he had pulled away.

"Tomorrow's not going to be awkward at all," she muttered sarcastically to herself as she climbed the stairs to her bedroom.

❧⋆❧

Chase felt his phone buzzing in his pocket. He took it out, Josh's number flashing on the caller ID.

"Hey," he said softly. His parents were just down the stairs, watching their evening television program. He'd come up to his childhood bedroom to pick up some things Fatima had left behind when she'd slept over the other week. "What's up?"

"I'm just checking in to see how you're doing," Josh replied. Chase could hear the unspoken apology in his voice about the ambush at dinner earlier.

"I'm alright," he reassured him.

"Just so we're clear, I tried to talk Kayla out of inviting her over tonight. I mean, I love Ally and all, but you're my best friend, and I know this time of year is hard for you and Fatima, and I just didn't want Ally to come in and complicate everything even more. I told Kayla we should just give you your space, but you know how she is. She just wants you to be happy."

"It's ok, I promise. I know you and Kayla were just looking out for me. And, as it turns out, it's not as hard seeing her back here again as I thought it would be." Even though he'd told Kayla just the other week that he didn't feel quite ready to date yet after Samar, he knew that both she and Josh worried about him, especially when the anniversary of her passing drew near. They'd both been so supportive of him since she had passed away, the two of them practically taking in Fatima as one of their own, helping him to raise her. He didn't think that he could've gotten through everything without the two of them.

"Oh yeah? Did something happen on that ride home we should know about?" He could hear the curiosity in Josh's voice.

"No, nothing like that," Chase reassured him. "And don't go mentioning anything about it to Kayla, either. It's not like Ally and I are going to jump into dating again."

"So, you've thought about the two of you dating again?" Josh pressed, a note of worry in his voice.

"What? No! I mean, she's only been in town for a day, for heaven's sake. It's not like I've had time to think about any of that. And it's not like that's even what I want, right now." His tone may have been indignant at the suggestion, but Chase knew, deep down, that he had briefly thought about it and the idea hadn't exactly seemed as outrageous to him as he was making it sound now. "No, I just mean that it was nice to see that Ally's really much the same person as she was before she left. She hasn't gotten caught up in all that fame and stardom and stuff. She's still her, the way I remember her. Being gone all this time, I was worried she would lose that part of her. It was nice to see that I was wrong."

Josh was skeptically silent, and Chase could feel him judging his response.

"Oh, don't be like that," Chase chastised him. "I promise: I have no plans to get back with Ally ever again."

He inadvertently felt his gaze drawn to the window, where he could see Ally's form moving behind the

Yours for the Holiday

curtain of her bedroom window.

"Good. Because the last thing we all need right now is more Ally drama in our lives. You've moved on, she's moved on. Let's just try to get through the holidays without anyone falling in love with anyone else again, ok?"

Moved on.

Had he moved on? He wasn't so sure. Seeing her tonight had taken him completely off-guard, dredging up old feelings even after all this time apart. And, if he was being honest with himself, Chase was afraid of how it made him feel when he was around her again. The whole ride home, all he'd wanted to do was ask her to pull the car over so he could kiss her. But when she was telling him about her life in L.A., and the struggle she was having trying to decide whether or not to come home, he'd surprised himself by saying that she should go back and keep pursuing her dreams, even though everything inside of him was screaming for him to tell her to come back home. To come back to *him*.

Why did he do it? It was the question he'd been asking himself ever since the words had come out of his mouth. He'd done it, he supposed, because he'd known that if he asked her to stay for him, she'd have only ended up resenting him in the end. Maybe it would take years, decades even, but eventually he would catch her wondering what her life could have been like if only she'd just hung in there a little longer and gave her acting career another shot, and Chase wasn't sure he could live with the thought of being the person who took that dream from her. It's why he'd let her go the first time, because he couldn't be the one to do that to her, even though it cost him everything to say it to her.

"I promise," Chase confirmed. He could hear

Josh heave a sigh of relief.

"Well, if I'd have known that being around Ally would make you this calm, I wouldn't have been worried so much about the two of you working on the dance together."

"Everything's going to be fine. And I was the one who asked her to help," he reminded him.

"Good, because it kind of seems like the Christmas dance depends on the two of you working well together," Josh pointed out. "The residents are looking forward to this, so I don't want anything to screw it up."

"We'll both be on our best behaviour, I promise. Look, I've got to head out, but Ally and I have got this. Nothing to worry about." As he hung up the phone, Chase hoped it was true.

Chapter Five

Ally ambled down the stairs the next morning, still bleary-eyed, where she was welcomed by her mother and sister.

"So, how was your night with Chase?"

"How'd you…?" she began.

"Saw you in the driveway talking to him last night as you dropped him off." She should've known. Her father had always joked that he and her mother had specifically chosen a bedroom at the front of the house because they'd wanted to be able to check that their daughters weren't trying to sneak out after curfew.

"Well, considering Kayla conveniently left out that he would also be at the dinner, it went well. Apparently, everyone forgot to let me know that he and Fatima live there, too." She glared at the both of them, taking a bite of the eggs her mother had placed in front of her.

"What's the deal with that, anyways? When I met her yesterday, I thought she was just the daughter of one of the nursing home employees or she was one of the kids he coaches, but when she was showing me around the house last night, there's all these pictures of her, and Chase, and another woman I'm assuming is Fatima's mom? And where was she last night? No one mentioned her."

An unexpectedly pained expression came over her mother's face, and Cassie went uncharacteristically quiet. "I think that's something that Chase should tell you himself."

It was clear her mother didn't want her to press the subject, but her reply only made Ally more interested. Obviously, there was something going on in Chase's life that no one wanted her to know about. She thought back to the night before when she and Chase had been sitting in the driveway and a similar pained look had come across his face, when they'd talked about their six years apart. She wondered if that had something to do with the matter at hand.

"Well," her mother started, visibly trying to shake off the gloom which had descended on the conversation, "I just think it's great you and Chase are spending time together. You know, his mother and I always thought the two of you would get married one day."

"Oh, you don't say," Ally said, rolling her eyes, her tone dripping with sarcasm.

"So, when *are* you and Chase going to settle down, Al? Should we be expecting to plan a summer wedding?" Cassie teased her.

"What about the fall? It's so pretty in the fall." Ally noted her mother's wistful tone and knew she wasn't entirely joking.

Yours for the Holiday

"We are *not* a couple. I'm just helping him with the Christmas Eve dance, is all. It's no big deal."

"And would it be such a bad thing if the two of you were to get back together again?" her mother asked her point blank. Ally thought about it for a moment. Her mother and Liv both had a point: what was holding her back from trying things again with Chase?

Because he wants more than just a week-long fling, and you know it. Her subconscious was ever the voice of reason.

"It would, actually," she whispered. She hadn't thought any of them had heard her. What was the point of starting something with him now? She didn't think she could do it to him all over again: get together with him again and then leave him for L.A. It had hurt enough the first time.

"Yeah, handsome, talented, great with kids and old folks alike… what's not to hate about him?" Cassie continued, ignoring the look that had come across Ally's face.

"Don't forget charitable," her mother pointed out. "He's not only throwing a dance for the seniors and their families, but he's also collecting donations for those who can't afford groceries this winter. He's a total monster."

They had a point: Chase was a wonderful person and a great catch for any lucky person fortunate enough to find themselves in love with him. But that was the problem. He was too good for the likes of her. She'd only end up hurting him again. Instead of pushing the two of them together, her family were only giving her more reasons why the two of them couldn't get back together.

"And I'm sure he'll make a fine husband… for someone else," Ally said, her tone a little sharper than she'd intended it to be. Cassie looked like she was about to give one of her usual retorts, but her mother gave her a look that stopped her.

"I think I'm going to go upstairs and lie down for a bit," Ally announced, even though she'd just gotten up and was still in her pyjamas. "I think the jet lag is still catching up to me."

For once, her mother didn't press her on it. "Of course, dear."

Ally headed up to her room and threw herself onto the bed, laying her head upon the pillow, but she wasn't tired. She sat up in bed and decided to video chat with Liv.

"Hey, you," Liv greeted her.

"Hey yourself."

"How is Vermont today?" Ally asked, noticing that Liv was currently curled up in front of a great stone fireplace, looking quite cozy.

"Well, there's no little ring-sized boxes under the Christmas tree yet, if that's what you're asking." To make her point, Liv turned her phone around to show her the Christmas tree they'd set up on the opposite side of the living room. There was a nice stack of presents wrapped in red and gold paper under the tree.

"Do you really think that Jackson would give away the surprise by just putting it out there for you to find it before he's ready?" Ally asked her, arching an eyebrow.

"I suppose not," Liv pouted. "But I was kind of hoping to at least see some hint of it. I'm beginning to think I got this whole thing wrong and got my hopes up for nothing. Maybe this trip was just that: a nice little Christmas getaway for the two of us. Maybe I was reading too much into it."

Yours for the Holiday

Ally felt for her friend. They'd all been there at one time or another in a relationship, reading too much into a gesture or something that was said. She didn't say this to Liv, of course, because she had been keeping Jackson's secret about proposing to her on this trip.

"Well, don't give up hope just yet," she encouraged. "There's still a few days left until Christmas Day. I'm sure Jackson's just waiting for the right time. Try not to worry about it. I'm sure you'll get your Christmas wish."

"You're right. I'm just being maudlin. So, tell me how things are going for you and that handsome high-school sweetheart of yours? Have the two of you found your way under the mistletoe yet? And by 'mistletoe' I mean, of course…"

"Yes, yes. I know what you mean," Ally said quickly, her cheeks reddening.

Liv smiled devilishly at her. "Well?" she pressed.

"No, nothing's happened. I went to dinner last night with a couple of friends at their place, and apparently, he lives there, too."

Liv's brow furrowed gracefully. "So, you two ended up having dinner together?" Her look changed from one of confusion to one of romantic possibilities.

"No, we did not. I mean, we did, but it wasn't like that," she quickly corrected her. "Josh and Kayla were there, and so was that ten-year-old girl I told you about yesterday.

"So, your friends adopted a kid, and you didn't know about it?"

"No, I think she's connected to Chase in some way but when I tried to ask my mom and sister about it at breakfast, they clammed up like it's some big secret."

She watched as Liv sat up and leaned closer to the

screen, intrigued. "That's kinda random, some kid living with him... Was he married to her mom or something?"

"I don't know. I don't know anything about her mom, other than some photos I saw in the house last night that I think are of her when Fatima was giving me a tour last night. I don't even know her name."

"Well, what else did you see when you were snooping around? Were there any signs of a woman living there?"

"I wasn't snooping around." Ally was slightly offended at the implication. "Fatima was giving me a tour of the house, and what was I supposed to find exactly?"

"I don't know... anything that might indicate if she was living there, or where she might be? Did you notice another toothbrush in the bathroom? Did you notice any of her clothes in his bedroom?"

"I didn't go into their bathroom, or his bedroom." Ally was quick to dispel any thoughts Liv might have about her and Chase sneaking off to his room together. "I don't know... I don't think saw any signs of her living there with them."

"Curiouser and curiouser," Liv said, quoting Alice in Wonderland.

"I know, right? I'm not sure what to think of it all."

"Well, I still think you should get on that," Liv commanded. "What are you waiting for?"

Ally squirmed under her gaze. "Chase is just not that kind of guy. He's just not the kind of guy to have a casual fling. I'd just end up hurting him again."

Liv gave her a pointed look. "Everyone's that kind of guy, Ally."

"Maybe in L.A.," she conceded. "But not here. Besides, if we did, the whole town would know about it within the hour, and it would just make everything so awkward."

Liv looked at her sympathetically. "Have you tried asking him what he wants? Maybe he's changed since the last time the two of you dated. Maybe he's not the same kind of person as he was back in high school."

"He isn't the same person," Ally agreed, thinking about how much more grown up he'd seemed since the two of them had reconnected. "But who he is, fundamentally... that hasn't changed about him. He's still the kind of guy who wants to give his whole heart to one woman, settle down, and start a family. He isn't the kind of guy who wants a casual fling with his ex-girlfriend who's going to be leaving in a few days."

"Look, all of that may be true, but you won't know unless you talk to him, will you?"

Ally sighed. She was hoping to get moral support on this instead of another lecture on how she should bootycall Chase. She glanced over at the radio clock by her bed.

"Oh, shoot! I'm going to have to run. I promised Chase I'd meet with him and Fatima today to help plan the dance. I need to get dressed and head out. I'm sorry to cut this short."

"Uh, huh. And this has nothing to do with the fact that this conversation makes you uncomfortable, at all," Liv said, her tone skeptical.

"Sorry! Gotta run! Love you!" Ally hurriedly closed her computer, grateful to be ending the conversation.

Erin Bowlen

As she rushed over to the nursing home, she mentally cursed herself for sleeping in so late. Now she wasn't going to have much time to spend with her grandmother before she, Chase, and Fatima had their lunch date to plan the dance. She hurriedly glanced at herself in the rearview mirror, hastily running her fingers through the fine strands of her brown hair in a desperate attempt to make herself look presentable.

"Well, I guess it'll have to do," she complained, getting out of the car and locking it behind her as she raced across the parking lot to get out of the cold.

"Hi, Grams! Sorry I'm late," Ally gave her a delicate hug, careful not to squeeze too tightly. She could feel every bone in her grandmother's shoulders through the fabric of her sweater. "I woke up late. I guess I'm still suffering from a bit of jet lag."

"That's alright, dear. You're here now." Her grandmother smiled at her and took her hand in hers as Ally settled herself on the chesterfield beside her.

"So, how are you feeling? How's your heart?" She gave her grandmother a concerned look.

"Oh, you know. The aches and pains are all part of getting old," her grandmother smiled ruefully. "Don't get old, by the way. It's not much fun. But my heart, it's happy to see you here."

Ally smiled sympathetically at her and squeezed her hand. "Aww, well, my heart is happy to see you too."

Her grandmother smiled at her, then turned her attention to the door. "Ah, I see. I'm not the only one you came to visit today." She nodded her head in the direction of the door. Ally turned around and saw Chase standing there. "I knew you couldn't be coming here just to visit little ol' me," her grandmother smiled at her devilishly.

Yours for the Holiday

"What? No... Grams!" Ally glanced between Chase and her grandmother, her face becoming flushed.

"It's fine, dear," her grandmother reassured her, patting her on the knee. "I know you two have the Christmas Eve dance to plan. You three go on and have fun now." Her grandmother planted a quick kiss on Ally's forehead before heading back to her room.

"So, should we get a start on it, then?" he asked her, pointing toward the front door.

Ally took his hand as she rose from her seat and let him lead her out to his warmed-up truck, where Fatima was waiting for them.

"I can't believe you still have this old thing." She gawked at his old beater of a truck that he'd had since high school. Road salt stained its underbelly, and she carefully maneuvered herself inside, trying not to get her clothes dirty.

"This old girl?" he asked, patting the dashboard lovingly. "I'd never get rid of her."

"It was falling apart back in high school," she replied, her tone incredulous. "Are you sure it's going to make it down the road? And why do guys always have to give their things feminine pronouns? It's not a person, it's a thing."

"A man has a special relationship with his vehicle," Chase replied, his tone all seriousness. "It's sacred."

Ally rolled her eyes and gave Fatima a knowing look. "Well, let's get this show on the road; if it will even get us where we're going..." she said. Her tone was dubious, demonstrating that she didn't believe it would make it five feet, let alone down the road to the diner.

Chase put the truck in drive. It lurched forward, stalled, then sputtered and groaned before coming back to life again.

"See? Perfectly fine." He patted the dashboard before putting the truck in drive. Ally and Fatima both gave him skeptical looks as they headed down to the diner.

As they entered the small, box-car style diner a few minutes later, she noticed that there were only two regulars sitting at the far end of the counter. The place hadn't changed one bit in the last six years. The same formica countertop, the same eight red leather, 1950's-style bar stools, the same photographs hanging on the wood-panelled walls. It was a miracle that the place still flew largely under the radar of Fredericton's foodies; with so many restaurants to choose from in such a small city, most people overlooked the tiny north-side diner, which was totally their loss, in Ally's opinion.

"Hey there, Fatima! What can I get for you and your friend?" the server asked, approaching Ally and Fatima's end of the counter. She gave Ally a funny look before asking, "Do I know you from somewhere?"

"Ally's a famous actress," Fatima proudly announced.

"Oh really? Wow!"

"Well, I'm not famous yet," Ally replied, trying to temper expectations.

"She was in magazines for this makeup campaign," Fatima continued, ignoring her.

"Hmm... I don't think I know you from movies or magazines... Wait, I've got it! You used to come here a few years back, didn't you? With Chase Cormier, right? I suppose that makes sense since you're here with this one," she winked at Fatima. "Large Caesar salad with grilled chicken and a coke?"

Ally was shocked. "Yeah, that's me. I can't believe you remember that!"

Yours for the Holiday

The server smiled, pleased at her recollection. "Always had a mind for recognizing faces." She placed a menu in front of her. "Can't remember names for the life of me, but faces and orders, I'd recognize them from anywhere. So, you joining Chase and Fatima today, then?"

"Yeah, we're having a lunch meeting."

The server nodded. "He always comes in for your usual lunch time. Haven't seen you here in quite awhile, though."

"I've been away for a few years. Wait, so you're saying that Chase has been coming here for lunch since we were in high school?"

"Yep, every day for one o'clock, like clock-work," the server replied cheerily. "A BLT on white with half fries/half onion rings, and an iced tea. Always packs the onion rings to go."

It had long been Chase's lunch order. He would always get half-and-half and give her the onion rings because she always wanted something greasy to balance out her salad. She felt strangely touched that he hadn't changed his order in all this time, even though she'd no longer been there to eat the onion rings.

"Chase!" the server smiled in greeting at him, the little bell above the door ringing as he entered.

"Lou." Chase leaned across the countertop and kissed the older woman on the cheek. "How are you today?"

"Oh, same ol', same ol'," she replied, but appeared pleased he'd asked, nonetheless.

"Did you two order, yet?" he asked, turning to her and Fatima.

"Um… no," she said, looking down at the menu. "I wasn't sure if you wanted your usual or something different this time."

"You remember my usual after all this time?" he asked, seemingly surprised and delighted at the thought.

"Well, I had a bit of help, remembering." She winked at Lou and Fatima. "BLT on white with half fries/half onion rings, right?"

"That's the one. I'll have that, Lou. What about you, kiddo?"

"I'll have my usual, too, Lou, please and thank you," Fatima replied. "Hey! That rhymes!"

"You're a poet and didn't know it," Chase teased her, tweaking her nose as she giggled.

"And for you, hun?" Lou looked at her expectantly.

"I guess I'll have my usual too," Ally said, handing her the menu.

"It's nice to see you with some company," Lou told Chase, setting paper placemats and their drinks in front of them. "Your orders will be right up." She disappeared into the back, giving them some privacy.

"So…" Chase started. "Where should we begin?"

Ally brought out her green notebook and Chase smiled at it.

"Well, if I'd known we were getting the Great Ideas notebook out, then I'd have made sure that Fatima and I came a lot more prepared for this meeting," he teased.

"No, you wouldn't have," she teased him back. "Just in case you didn't already know, Fatima, Chase never plans for anything."

"Oh, I know," Fatima teased back. "So, what's a Great Ideas notebook? It looks like just a regular notebook to me."

"Oh no. This is no ordinary notebook," Chase replied. "It may look all plain and normal on the outside,

Yours for the Holiday

but it's what's on the inside that counts." Ally felt butterflies in her stomach under his warm gaze.

"Of course, the Great Ideas notebook hasn't always looked like this. You remember that sparkly, aquamarine one your Grams got you that Christmas when we were ten?"

Ally nodded. "I can't believe you remember that!"

"That was the first Great Ideas notebook," Chase told Fatima, leaning in conspiratorially. "She was supposed to use it as a diary, but Ally here decided that was too conventional, and so she started filling it with all these drawings and snippets of poems and ideas she'd come up with. Didn't you plan our wedding in one of these notebooks?"

Ally felt her face go bright red. "Maybe…"

"You two were going to get married?" Fatima asked. Her tone was shocked, but she seemed to like this idea.

"Yes, she did. When we were twelve, I think? I remember we were walking along the hallway at school when it fell out of her bookbag and opened right up to all these beautiful sketches of the gown she was going to wear, and the bridesmaids' dresses…"

"I was *so* embarrassed!" Ally hid her face in her hands at the memory. She'd definitely never intended for him to see that.

"What did it look like? The dress?"

"All I remember is that it was white and poufy," Chase said, taking a sip of his water.

"I can't imagine you in a poufy dress," Fatima replied, sounding skeptical.

"Neither can I," Ally admitted, finally lifting her head. "But when I wasn't much older than you are, it was what I thought I wanted."

"So, you've always had a Great Ideas journal, then?"

"Well, I haven't used one in awhile," she admitted. A look passed between her and Chase. She'd given up on using her journal in her senior year of high school, right after she'd started planning her move to Los Angeles. She'd actually forgotten about the journals until she'd been rifling through her desk drawer last night and had stumbled upon it, and the urge to plan this dance with him had just come over her, and she'd started writing everything down.

"Well, that's ok," Fatima reassured her. "So, what ideas did you come up with? Can I have a look?"

"Of course," Ally smiled at her. "So, I was thinking we'd go with a Winter Wonderland theme." She opened the notebook so they both could see.

"Sounds... over the top," Chase said cautiously. "I was thinking this would be just a dance with some family and friends of our residents."

"Typical dude." Ally rolled her eyes at him. "You can't just put on some Christmas music and call it a dance."

"Yeah, Chase," Fatima echoed the sentiment. "I think a Winter Wonderland sounds magical! See? I told you Ally would know how to plan a party!"

"What's wrong with my idea?" Chase asked, his tone perplexed.

"Ha, ha," she said, knowing he was only joking. "Anyways, if you want this to be special for everyone, then you need to put some effort into it. You need to do some planning."

"This is why I have the two of *you*," he pointed out, giving her one of those wonderfully charming smiles that turned her insides all warm and fuzzy.

Yours for the Holiday

"Here's a playlist of classic Christmas tunes I thought we could use." She handed him a piece of paper with the selection of songs she'd written down. "I thought we could put them on an iPod and just hook it up to some speakers, and that way we don't need to hire a band or anything."

"That's good, because I asked Josh what our budget for this dance is, and he just chuckled. We barely have enough money for a few decorations."

"I figured you'd say that. So, speaking of decorations, I was thinking that we should keep it simple, but classy." She pointed to the pages where she'd sketched out some simple designs using paper streamers and twinkling lights.

"Wow, that looks amazing." He held his hand out to take a closer look, their fingers brushing as she handed him the book. Their eyes locked for a moment, and the whole world around them seemed to fade away.

"And here are your orders," Lou suddenly announced, interrupting the moment. Ally felt jolted back to the present as Chase broke off his gaze and carefully put the notebook to one side. "Just holler if you need anything else."

"Thanks Lou," Chase called out to her as she disappeared to the back of the diner again. The three of them ate in a comfortable silence for a few minutes. As Ally took a bite of her salad, she thought she might die and go to heaven.

"Oh my God, this is still the best chicken Caesar I've ever tasted," she exclaimed.

Chase grinned at her. "Even better than mine?"

Ally rolled her eyes at him. "Nothing's better than your cooking." She couldn't help but notice how pleased Chase seemed at her compliment. "You know, I still think you could totally open up your own restaurant."

"Do you know how hard it is to open a restaurant here in Fredericton? For a city of fifty thousand, there's a surprisingly high number of restaurants. It's hard to compete. People like their tried-and-true places."

She rolled her eyes at his casual dismissiveness. "That's always been your problem."

"What has?"

"One: you always give up on yourself too quickly. And two, you're afraid of a little competition."

"That's two problems," Fatima piped up.

"What?"

"You said 'That's always been your problem,' meaning that Chase only had one problem, but you just named two."

"Ok, so two problems," she replied, smiling at her. "My point is: you need to stop being afraid all the time and just go for things. If I worried about the competition all the time, I'd never go to another audition again."

She noticed he bristled at her words, but she wasn't going to be put off from making her point just because he didn't like being challenged. Chase had always been afraid to take life by the horns and she felt it was time to point it out.

"For example, when we were in high school, you loved baseball, and you were great at it. But you never took it seriously because you didn't want to deal with the competition. And now what, hmm? You plan to work at the nursing home for the rest of your life?"

"I like working at the nursing home." Chase's tone was brusque. "Six years is a long time to be away, Ally; people change, dreams change. You'd know that if you'd been here."

His words stung, but she couldn't deny the truth

Yours for the Holiday

of them. She was the one who'd left, and she couldn't expect him to have stayed the same all this time. The fact that they were sitting here with Fatima was proof of that. Sensing that she'd made things incredibly awkward, she turned her attention back to her food until she noticed him moving his plate closer to her out of the corner of her eye.

"Onion ring?" he asked, turning the plate towards her so she could grab one. She took the peace offering, showing him she didn't resent him for his gruff tone before.

"So, I reached out to the Food Bank this morning, and here's the list of all the non-perishable items they need at the moment." She placed the list in front of Chase and Fatima, getting back to the matter at hand.

"This is great. Thanks for doing that."

"I was thinking that we should put the this list up on the noticeboard near the front door so that the families can take a look at it before the dance and know what to bring."

"You're amazing." She felt a rush of joy when he said it, her face beaming with pride.

"You're welcome. It was nothing," she blushed, tucking a strand of her dark brown hair behind her ear. She didn't know why, but it made her both thrilled and embarrassed at the attention Chase was giving her. She hadn't felt like this since she was back in high school. She cleared her throat. "So, we should go and buy the decorations soon, like tomorrow or the next day. Most of the best decorations will already have been bought up by people who, you know, think of these things ahead of time."

She winked at him in amusement.

"Ha, ha," Chase retorted. "Why don't the three of us go today after we're done here?"

"Don't you have to get back to work? And don't you have to go to school?" she asked, looking at the both of them.

Chase shrugged. "I'll text Josh and let him know we'll be out for the afternoon. Besides, this is for work, so it counts as work."

"And I'm on Christmas break," Fatima pointed out.

"Well, today it is, then." They finished their meals. When they were done, Ally dug out her wallet.

"I got this," Chase said, taking the cheque from Lou and handing her his credit card.

"You always have to be chivalrous." Ally rolled her eyes, but secretly, she was pleased.

"You ate the onion rings this time," Lou looked at him, surprised.

"Yeah, I guess I found someone to share them with." He winked at Ally and that feeling of butterflies returned to her stomach. She glanced away, catching Fatima's eye, noticing how the young girl was beaming at this little exchange. After settling the bill, Chase and Ally headed outside. He walked over with her to the passenger side, opening the door and holding it for her as she and Fatima hopped inside.

"Brr!" she exclaimed, a chill running down her spine as he opened the driver's side door and got in.

"Here we go." Chase turned on the truck and put the heat on full blast. The three of them drove to the store in silence for a few minutes, listening to the Christmas music on the radio. Just as the first few bars of Mariah Carey's "All I Want for Christmas" came on, Chase turned the radio off.

"What have you got against Mariah?" Ally asked. Personally, she'd always liked the upbeat tune.

Yours for the Holiday

"Nothing," Chase replied.

"I love this song!" Fatima reached out and turned the volume up again. "Chase says I'm going to wear out the stereo listening to it." She smirked at him.

"Tom used to say the same thing about me," Ally replied, without thinking.

"I don't mind the song, but it's not the only Christmas song I want to listen to. So, Tom, eh? Does that mean you're seeing someone out in L.A.?"

She noticed the way he'd tried to make the question seem totally normal, but the higher pitch of his voice betrayed him. He clearly didn't want to know any more about her love life than she wanted to know about his. Fatima glanced between the two of them, noticing this little exchange.

"No," Ally replied, honestly. He sighed audibly in relief, and it was all Ally could do to stop herself from chuckling.

"I was seeing someone for awhile, but we ended things a few weeks ago." Just mentioning Tom brought up a whole host of feelings she didn't want to be having right now in front of Chase or Fatima. She'd thought that when she and Tom had ended things, she'd put these feelings to rest, but seeing him the other day with his new girlfriend had stung more than she'd been willing to admit at the time.

"I'm sorry," he said, glancing over at her. She must've had a pained expression on her face because his own was more sympathetic than she would've expected.

"Oh, it's fine." She dismissed his worries with a wave of her hand, but that still didn't stop her from feeling uneasy talking about it with him. "He's with someone new now."

"That... wow, that's quick." Chase seemed

surprised by this bit of information.

"Yeah, I know, right?" Ally admitted before she could stop herself. "And it's kind of serious, too. Just before I left L.A., I bumped into him and his new girlfriend and he's taking her to Hawaii for the holiday he was supposed to be going on with me." She couldn't help but have a bit of an edge in her voice. She didn't know why she was telling them all of this; maybe it was that, since she'd been back, for all the romantic awkwardness between them, there was still that easy friendship they used to have. That had been the hardest part about their breakup because it hadn't just been a normal breakup between her and a guy she'd liked; she'd also been breaking up with one of her best friends.

"What the...? The..." Chase spluttered, trying to come up with the right word.

"Jerk?" Fatima supplied, surprising the both of them.

"There's a few choice things I'd like to call that guy, and jerk's the mildest one." He cleared his throat. "Well, in any case, it sounds like you're better off without him. He clearly doesn't know what he's lost." He gave her a look, then, like he knew exactly what he'd lost.

"Thanks," she replied, looking out the window, trying to hide the telltale emotions on her face. "Oh, look! There's a spot over there." She pointed to an empty parking spot near the store entrance.

Chase parked the car, and the three of them headed inside. The rush of warm air from the *whoosh!* of the automatic doors made her loosen her scarf. As they entered the store, she was greeted by a huge cardboard cut-out of herself from the modelling gig she'd had a few months before.

"Look, Ally! It's you!" Fatima exclaimed.

"Oh God," she muttered under her breath and quickly turned down one of the aisles away from the make-up section, hoping no one had seen her. She noticed there were only two teenaged girls in that section, and both seemed to be glued to their cellphones.

"So, it is!" Chase said, laughing a bit at the embarrassed look on her face.

"Come away from there!" she hissed at them both.

"Oh, come on. Don't tell me now that you've become shy?" he teased her.

"No, it's just… weird," she admitted. "I'm not used to seeing myself in life-sized advertisements."

"That's probably a good thing. If you were, then I'd have to refer you to a shrink for narcissistic personality disorder." She gave him a withering look before heading down the aisle with the decorations.

"I think you look really pretty in that photo," Fatima said, following along behind her.

"It's a pretty picture and all, but I prefer the real Ally," Chase said suddenly. "That version's a little too airbrushed for my taste." His body language indicated he was trying to be off-hand with his comment, but there was something in his tone that said he was being deliberate with his words.

Ally self-consciously tucked a strand of dark-brown hair behind her ear. "Chase Cormier, was that another compliment?" she teased. She didn't know how to take him seriously at the moment. She was afraid of what it would mean if she did. "You're unusually full of them today."

"Well, what can I say? You make it easy to be complimentary when it's the truth." She coughed politely, trying to focus on the decorations in front of them.

"What about this?" he asked, holding up some green and red tinsel once they'd found the decorations aisle. "Can't have too much tinsel."

"Says the guy with terrible taste in holiday décor, eh Fatima?" she teased, picking up some red and green paper streamers instead. "How about these instead?"

"These are pretty," Fatima agreed.

"Besides, if you go with the tinsel, you'll be cleaning up strands of it all year long, and it's terrible for the environment."

"Think about the environment, Chase!" Fatima begged.

"Alright, then," Chase caved into the pressure.

"OMG," Ally overheard the two girls from earlier whisper a few feet in front of them, momentarily distracting her. They were glancing up and down from their cellphones and back at her again. Although she wasn't famous in a place like Los Angeles by any means, Ally had seen it happen enough times to others to know when she was being recognized. In a place as small as Fredericton, where everyone knew everyone, it had been bound to happen sooner or later. The two teenagers slowly approached her.

"Are you Ally Hayes?" one of them asked nervously.

"She sure is!" Fatima supplied cheerfully.

"Can we get a selfie?" the second one asked.

"It's not every day that someone from here goes and becomes famous!" the first one explained.

"Of course," Ally replied. The three young women crowded in together as one of the teens held up their phone to take the picture.

"Here, I'll take it." Chase held his hand out to her, and she gave her phone to him. "Everyone say 'cheese!'"

Yours for the Holiday

Ally gave her best practiced smile, the teens beaming on either side of her.

"Thanks so much!" they chorused and headed off back towards the parking lot.

"That was *so* cool! I told you that you were famous!" Fatima walked along the aisle, clearly thrilled that she was in the company of someone she thought was cool.

Ally turned and looked at Chase, who had a curious expression on his face. "What?"

"Nothing," he said, following Fatima with their shopping cart.

She rolled her eyes at him, knowing that he was lying. "You hate all that, don't you?"

"Hate what?"

"The... what did you used to call it? The circus that comes with fame?" She distinctly remembered a conversation between the two of them when they were in high school where he'd gone on and on about how he'd never be able to cope with the attention that comes with fame. She'd known then – even if she hadn't been willing to admit it to herself – that Chase would never follow her out to Los Angeles and live that kind of life with her. That was when things had ended between the two of them.

"No, I don't hate it. What would make you think that?"

She looked at him with a bit of surprise. "It's just... well, you always used to flinch every time I brought up L.A."

Chase frowned at this. "I'm not going to pretend like I wasn't hurt when you left, and I'm not saying that I'd want that kind of life for myself, but that doesn't mean that I hate that L.A.'s a part of you now. Acting makes you happy, and I like seeing you happy."

He gave her a small smile then, one that warmed her heart more than she could put into words. She very much wanted to reach up and kiss him right here in the middle of the aisle, spectators be damned. But she knew she couldn't put him through the kind of lifestyle she hoped to live. The two of them were on separate paths, and she'd been the one to set them onto their current course and she couldn't take it back. She knew she couldn't have them both: Chase and acting, and it wasn't fair to her or Chase to think otherwise.

After the moment passed, she steered them in the direction of the checkout and grabbed the bags of decorations while Chase paid for them. "Well, it's basically the end of the day. I don't think there's much point in going back to the office now. Would you like me to drop you off at your parents' place? Fatima and I have to head that way anyways, so it wouldn't be a problem."

"What about my mom's car? I left it back at the nursing home."

Chase waved his hand as if to dismiss her worry. "It'll be fine there overnight. We were planning to spend the night at my parents' place; I can take you in, in the morning, and then you can spend more time with your Grams."

"Sure. Thanks, that'd be nice."

The three of them spent the rest of the drive in a comfortable silence. As they pulled up in front of the Cormiers' house, Ally noticed that there were some children from the block playing hockey at the foot of Baseball Hill. Chase had barely pulled the truck to a stop before Fatima opened the door and hopped out.

"Woah, there. What have I said about making sure the truck is turned off before you get out?" he asked, his tone a touch stern.

"Can I go and play with them?" she asked sweetly.

"What about these bags? They aren't going to carry themselves in."

Fatima pouted, but reached in and grabbed the bags. "Ok."

"Thank you!" he called to her as she scampered inside with them. "So, I'll pick you up tomorrow morning before work so we can head back to the nursing home and maybe get in some decorating?" he asked, turning to Ally.

"It's a date." She saw Chase's eyes widen in surprise. "No, not a date, I mean… sorry, like, the expression…"

Chase's eyes filled with mirth. "I know what you meant." He chuckled. "See you tomorrow."

Chapter Six

Ally heard the knock on the front door like it was some far-off bird tapping against her window. She grumbled at its intrusion into her sleep and pulled the thick comforter over her face, hoping it might encourage whomever it was to go away.

"Ally!" her mother called up the stairs. "Ally?"

Throwing the covers off her and flipping onto her back, Ally grumbled as she reluctantly got out of bed and headed towards the top of the stairs.

"Wha-?" she mumbled, rubbing the sleep from her eyes.

"There you are, sleepy-head. Chase is here for you." Her mother nodded toward the front door.

Ally's mind jolted out of its half-asleep state when she realized Chase was standing in the front doorway, looking up at her. She was suddenly very aware that she

Yours for the Holiday

was still in her pyjamas, her hair a rat's nest, with not a stitch of make-up on. She self-consciously wrapped her arms across her chest, trying not to give him a view of her cleavage in her tank top.

"Oh, um, hi, good morning," she greeted him, trying not to sound as awkward as she felt.

"Good morning," he chuckled. "I thought you, me, and Fatima could get some breakfast together before heading over to the nursing home to get started with the decorating," he explained. "But if you're still sleeping..."

"No, no. Give me ten minutes and I'll be right down." She raced to the bathroom, caught a glimpse of herself in the mirror, and winced.

"Well, we'll just have to work with what we got," she muttered to herself as she hastily brushed her teeth, washed her face, and pulled her tousled hair up into a high bun. She quickly put on some light make-up, just enough to hopefully give her that fresh morning glow, and ran to her bedroom, looking for her clothes. She finally settled on a pair of black skinny jeans and a red-and-black plaid shirt. She hurried down the steps two at a time and stood in front of Chase.

"Ta da!" she said, like she had just done some kind of magic trick.

"One minute to spare. I'm impressed." Chase smiled at her. "Now hurry up. You're going to make me late for work. And Fatima says she's *starving* and she may waste away." He emulated the young girl's tone.

Ally smiled at him as she followed him outside to his truck. "Hey Fatima!"

"Ally!" The young girl's enthusiasm was a bit too chirpy for this time of the morning, considering that Ally was still a little sleepy, but nevertheless, she couldn't help but smile at her. She climbed into the passenger seat of

Chase's truck and the three of them headed for the Tim Hortons.

"A large double-double, a large candy cane hot chocolate, an apple juice, half a dozen muffins, and your largest box of doughnuts, please," Chase told the young teenager serving them at the drive-thru.

"All that food for the three of us?" Ally asked, carefully placing their drinks in the truck's cupholders and handing Fatima her bottle of apple juice.

"Well, the drinks and muffins are for us," he said, handing her the rest of their order. "And I thought it would be nice to bring the residents a little treat this morning. It's nearly Christmas, after all." He winked at her as he pulled out of the drive-thru and back onto the street, heading for the nursing home.

"Alright," he said, a few minutes later, parking the truck. "Fatima, why don't you take the muffins and my keys, and go open my office for me, ok?"

"Ok!" She took the keys and the box of muffins, scampering towards Chase's office.

"You want to carry the drinks or the doughnuts?" he asked.

"Doughnuts," she replied. "I don't trust myself not to spill the drinks, and I know how fussy you are about your coffee."

"That I am," he said with all seriousness, carefully balancing their drinks as he closed the truck door with his hip, the two of them heading inside. When they got to Chase's office, Fatima had already begun tucking into her muffin.

"I guess someone couldn't wait for the rest of us," Chase teased her.

"I told you I was starving!" She took a big mouthful of chocolate chip muffin, emphasizing her point.

Yours for the Holiday

"Ok, but don't eat it so fast," he gently chastised. "Here, why don't you take your muffins and apple juice into the rec room. I'm sure everyone will be thrilled to see you." Fatima took the blueberry muffin he offered her and followed him out the door.

"I'll be right back," he told Ally, following Fatima out with the doughnuts for the residents.

She nodded, picking up her hot chocolate, feeling the hot paper cup warm on her fingertips.

"Mmhmm." She breathed in its peppermint scent, letting the drink warm her insides as she took a sip. "I've forgotten how good Tim Hortons' food is."

She heard Chase's chuckle behind her as he returned to his office a moment later. He sat down in his chair, taking a sip of his coffee. "You're so going to be wired for the rest of the day with all that sugar."

"That is entirely your fault," she pointed out.

"Well, I know how much you used to love candy cane hot chocolate. I thought you might be missing it out in L.A." She nodded. While there were plenty of exciting new places to eat at in L.A., but sometimes she missed the familiarity of home.

"Would you like chocolate chip, carrot, blueberry, or mixed fruit?" he asked her, turning the box of muffins in her direction.

"Chocolate chip and carrot, please," she said, knowing that he preferred the fruit muffins. She reached across the desk, grabbing her muffins, bumping her elbow into the desk lamp, almost knocking it over.

"Sorry!" she exclaimed, as Chase reached out and expertly caught it with cat-like reflexes.

"No, I'm sorry," he said, looking embarrassed at the small space. "I know. It's a broom closet. To be honest, I don't normally tend to work in here. I'm usually out in the rec room with the residents. I really only come here when I have to get paperwork done."

Ally brushed away any worries with the wave of her hand. "It's fine. It's cozy."

She admired the photos on his walls, photos of Chase with his parents, Chase with Josh and Kayla, and Chase with Fatima and the woman she'd seen in the photos back at his house. She noticed one photo of him, Josh, Kayla, and her when they'd been children. They were standing by the banks of the Nashwaak River after having been tubing. They all had big grins on their faces.

"I remember this," she said, picking up the framed photo, careful not to knock anything else over. She stared down at her younger self.

"Yeah," he replied, grinning at her. "That was the day you fell out of your tube, and I had to dive in after you to rescue you."

She rolled her eyes at him. "You didn't rescue me. I'm an excellent swimmer. You almost brought the two of us down when you jumped in after me."

In truth, they were both right. Ally had accidentally fallen out of her tube and, knowing the swift current of the Nashwaak and how the river varied vastly in depth, she easily could have fallen into one of the deeper parts and been sucked under by the current. Chase had jumped in after her to make sure she was safe.

"Sure, you keep telling yourself that," he teased her, taking a bite of his muffin.

As she took another sip of her hot chocolate, her eyes alighted on the other photo on his desk. This one was also of the four of them, but from their high school years. She recognized it as having been taken at Grand Lake the night of their prom. The night that she and Chase had broken up. Seeing what she was looking at,

Yours for the Holiday

Chase cleared his throat.

"Should we go and check on Fatima?" he asked.

"Yeah, sure." She cleared her throat and leaned back in her chair. Getting up from her chair, she followed him out of his office to the rec room. "How are things going in here?"

"Fatima was just telling me all about how excited she is for Christmas," Ally's grandmother told her.

Fatima nodded her head enthusiastically. "But first we have the dance, and I'm really excited for that, too! Everyone is." Several of the seniors sitting at her grandmother's table nodded along with her.

"We're expecting it to be great." Her grandmother winked at her.

"So, no pressure then," Ally chuckled.

"Yeah, you really gotta make sure it doesn't suck," Fatima agreed.

"Well, you know, I was thinking that one way to make sure it doesn't suck is to have a Christmas tree," Chase interrupted. "In fact, Josh just texted to say that he and Kayla are out at the Christmas tree lot right now, and they wanted to know if we wanted to join them?"

Fatima looked excited. "Let's go!"

Ally chuckled at her as Fatima grabbed Chase's hand and began pulling him towards the door, Ally following on their heels.

ॐ

The air was heavy with the scent of pine trees as Ally emerged from Chase's truck. She took a deep breath, filling her lungs with the scent of home.

"C'mon, let's go!" Fatima bounced excitedly out

of the truck, heading straight for the Christmas tree farm. It was a family farm not far from Josh and Kayla's place that made a whole experience of Christmas tree shopping with pony rides for the kids.

"Alright, slow down," Chase told her as she bolted for the ponies.

"Can I ride the ponies? Please?"

"Alright, one go around, and then we need to find a tree!" he called after her, but she was already out of earshot.

Ally laughed. "Well, someone's excited."

"Yeah, I'm glad to see it. This time of year isn't easy for her."

Ally nodded, knowing he was referencing whatever had taken place during the six years that she'd been away. She wanted to ask him about it, to find out what the mystery was, but she remembered her mother's advice from the other day about letting Chase tell her in his own time. Instead, she walked over to the paddock where they were hosting the pony rides, joining Fatima in the line.

"Is there one you like?" she asked her.

"That one." She pointed to a gentle-looking Shetland pony.

"Good choice," the teenage girl operating the pony rides told her. "Bella's really sweet."

"Up you go." Ally watched as Chase held Fatima's hand so she could steady herself as she climbed onto Bella's back.

"All good?"

Fatima nodded excitedly. The teenaged girl double-checked her stirrups and her position in the saddle to ensure she was safe before taking Bella's halter and leading them around the paddock for a few turns.

"Are you getting photos?" Fatima called out from

Yours for the Holiday

the other side of the paddock.

"I'm taking loads of them!" Chase called back, clicking away with his phone. "That's a great one!"

He leaned over to let Ally have a look, close enough for her to feel his warm breath on her cheek.

"That *is* a great one," she confirmed, smiling at him. Her gaze lingered just a little longer than she'd meant it to. She diverted her attention back to Fatima.

"How was that?" she asked, as Fatima dismounted.

"Can I go again?"

"I think we'd better get that tree, don't you?" Chase asked her.

Fatima looked slightly disappointed, but quickly recovered. "Yeah, I guess so. Ally's grandmother said we needed to find the best one on the lot."

"That sounds like Grams. Well, let's get started, shall we?"

"Hey you three!" Ally turned around at the sound of Kayla's voice behind her.

"Hey there! Chase said you were both here."

"Yeah, well, when Josh mentioned that the nursing home needed a tree and Chase was planning to take you and Fatima out here to get one, I thought we'd better show up and help. You know what you two are like; you can't agree on anything, and I didn't want Fatima to have to referee all by herself."

"Hey, I take offense at that!" Ally remarked playfully. "Chase and I wouldn't disagree on anything, would we?"

"Nope. Complete agreement on everything," he teased, a wide grin on his face.

"See? Complete agreement. We can behave like adults." Kayla burst out laughing.

"What's so funny?" Josh asked, joining the group.

"Chase and Ally, and how they think they don't argue about literally everything."

Josh laughed uproariously. "That was a good one. I needed that laugh. Thanks."

"Oh stop! We're not that bad."

"I agree," Chase backed her up. "See? There's something else we agree on."

"Well, in that case, we better get started before that changes." They headed off in the direction of the tree stands.

"Ah, here we go." Chase moved towards a stand with tall, full evergreens.

"What about this one?" Ally pulled out a plump tree about the same height as her. Fatima pondered the tree. "It's a bit short."

Ally gasped dramatically. "Did she just call me short?" she asked Chase.

"I think she did. But, in all fairness, you are kinda short." Ally teasingly scoffed at this remark.

"Do you hear this?" she asked Kayla, who was an inch or two shorter than her.

Kayla nodded. "Oh yeah, I hear them and frankly, I'm a bit offended because we prefer vertically challenged."

"You two are silly," Fatima laughed at them as they continued down the path to look at more trees.

"Ok, here we go!" Chase lifted a tree that was a full head taller than his 5'11 frame.

"That is definitely better," Fatima agreed, looking up at the tree with wonderment. "I think this is the one!"

"You realize we have to get it through the front door, right?" Josh gave him a skeptical look. He and Chase were about the same height and build, and Ally could see he was sizing up exactly how the two of them were going to carry the tree from the truck to the rec room.

"Oh, it'll be fine," Chase dismissed his worries. "Have a little faith, would you?"

"I don't know…" Josh continued to look skeptical at his friend's plan.

"We'll put Kayla and Ally to work bringing it in." Kayla folded her arms over her chest, raising an eyebrow in his direction, silently regarding him.

"Oh, you will, will you?" Ally asked, mirroring her stance.

"Please? For the seniors?" He made that cute face he knew she couldn't resist, his big brown eyes going soft.

"Oh, alright," she caved in, rolling her eyes dramatically.

Chase grinned from ear to ear, pleased with having won her over. "Great. Josh, would you go and find the guy so we can pay him?" Josh looked around the lot, finding the elderly, grizzled man who operated the Christmas tree farm and headed off in his direction.

Ally caught Kayla smirking at her from the corner of her eye. "What?"

Kayla moved off to the side a bit, slightly out of earshot of Josh and Chase. "Nothing."

"Oh, come on. I remember that look all too well, and you've never once been shy in your life about having an opinion on something. Come on, out with it."

"It's just nice seeing you and Chase together again, acting like old times." Ally scoffed at the idea.

"So, you're saying that you agreed to help lug a Christmas tree around purely because it would be nice for the seniors at the nursing home and had nothing to do with the puppy dog look Chase was giving you?"

"Well, I'm a very generous person," Ally retorted.

"You may be a kind-hearted person, Al, but we both know that this is about more than just that. Just be careful, ok? It's fun to flirt and all, but you're only here for the holidays. I just wouldn't want Chase getting the wrong idea about what's going on. He had a really hard time after you left. I just don't want to see him hurt again." Ally didn't have time to reply because Josh and Chase had come over to where they were standing.

"I think we're going to put the tree in our truck," Josh told his fiancée. "It's got a bit more room than Chase's."

"Ok." She pulled out her keys. "Let's go take this into town."

"Look, Fatima. Looks like they've got some free hot chocolate set up over there. Would you like some?"

"Hmm… no," Fatima pondered the question. "Can I go with Josh and Kayla to bind the tree, though?"

"Of course! Just stick close to them, ok?"

"Ok!" she shouted over her shoulder, running to catch up to Kayla.

"Well, I'd like some hot chocolate. Is the offer is still open?"

"Après vous," Chase replied with the ease of someone raised in a bilingual household.

"Two hot chocolates, please."

"Here you go," the woman operating the makeshift stand handed them each a styrofoam cup. "Can I just say that you three make such a lovely family?"

"Oh, we're not…" Ally said at the same time as Chase replied with a simple, "Thanks."

The older woman had a slightly bemused look on her face. "Well, you three have a Merry Christmas," she replied before turning her attention to another family.

"You know, she was only trying to be nice," Chase said as they moved to rejoin Josh, Kayla, and Fatima, who were watching the tree as it was bound up in twine.

"Yeah, I know. I just didn't want to give the wrong impression is all," she said, remembering what Kayla had said earlier about leading him on. She'd been right; it had felt like old times being back here again, but that meant it was also all too easy for the two of them to fall back into old patterns. She was leaving in less than a week. She couldn't give Chase the wrong idea about things.

"Well, should we get this show on the road, then?" Kayla asked as they rejoined the group.

"Let's," Ally said, heading into Chase's truck, and the five of them headed back into town.

⁂

"Oh, good Lord!" Ally exclaimed, as she and Kayla helped Chase and Josh carry the tree from his truck into the nursing home. "This thing weighs a ton!"

"But it'll look some pretty once it's all decorated," Chase reassured her, smiling. They managed to get it through the front doors of the building, the automatic doors trying to cut them off before they could properly enter the building.

"Now that is a proper Christmas tree," Cassie said proudly as they brought it into the rec room. Their grandmother nodded approvingly.

"Chase just had to pick the largest one on the lot, so it had better do," Ally teased, coming over to give her sister and grandmother a hug. She brushed a few pine needles that had transferred from her coat to her grandmother's shirt. "I didn't know you were coming over to visit Grams today."

"Mom asked if you and I would help her with some of the Christmas baking for the dance while she and Dad go to his company's party tonight. So, I stopped by to visit Grams while I was on my way to the grocery store to pick up some more supplies. There's supposed to be a big storm tonight, so she wants us to go now in case we get snowed in. You know how she is; always preparing for the worst."

The corners of Ally's mouth turned up in a half-smile. Their mother would have made the most excellent Girl Guide. She was always prepared for every eventuality. "Do you want some help with the groceries?"

"Nah, it's alright, if you've got stuff to do here."

"Does that mean we can decorate the tree now?" Fatima asked, her tone hopeful.

"We've got to unwrap it from the twine and let it out for the night so the branches have time to settle into place. But we can start decorating it tomorrow," Chase promised her, coming over to join the conversation. Fatima seemed like she thought she couldn't wait that long, but seemed resigned to the situation.

"Well, hey, the day's not entirely lost," Ally said, coming quickly to the rescue. "How would you like to come over to our place tonight and help Cassie and I with baking cookies for the dance?" She gave Cassie a questioning look, as if to ask if that was alright.

"Hey, that sounds like a brilliant plan!" her sister replied enthusiastically.

Fatima looked at Chase, hope filling her eyes. "Can I?"

Chase shrugged. "It's fine with me."

Yours for the Holiday

"Yes!" Ally, Chase, and Cassie smiled at her enthusiasm.

"Who knew baking cookies would be so popular?" Ally asked.

"I think it's more about the company," Chase replied, giving her a wink, making her blush. "But I think it's a little about the cookies, too," he quickly recovered.

Ally felt her cheeks going red when she noticed the knowing look that Cassie was giving the two of them. "Right, well, I guess we'll see you tonight, then?"

"I'll drop her off at your place around five?"

"Sounds good."

"You two be careful out there. That storm's going to be a big one," their grandmother warned.

"Really? It looks like it's not going to be as bad as the weather channel says," Cassie gently contradicted her.

"That not what these old bones are saying." Her grandmother idly massaged a sore muscle in her leg. "I wouldn't make any big plans to go out tonight. You tell your parents they might want to skip that party."

"I'm sure we'll all be fine, Grams," Ally reassured her. "Now, how about we go and get those groceries?" Ally linked arms with her sister, practically pulling her in the direction of the door.

"We've got time. You sure you wouldn't want to stay here a little longer and spend some more time planning the dance with Chase?" Cassie winked at her.

"Let's go!" Ally replied through clenched teeth, trying to keep a smile on her face in front of the others as she practically pushed her sister out of the room and towards the parking lot.

"Ok, ok! Sheesh! If I didn't know better, I would say that you're trying to run away from Chase," Cassie complained as they stepped out into the cool air.

"I'm not trying to get away from Chase," she snapped, but she knew the tone of her voice betrayed her. "I just want to get a move on before this storm comes." They both looked up at the sky. Although it was clear where they were at the moment, they both could see the big, dark grey clouds of the storm front moving in from the north.

"We've got plenty of time. Besides, I don't think it'll be as bad as Grams, or the weather people say. You know what the weather is like here in the Maritimes: wait five minutes and it'll change. Or, maybe you've forgotten what it's like having all that sunshine out in L.A. all the time." Cassie dismissed her excuses, but they both noticed a few snowflakes falling lightly around them. "Ok, maybe you've got a point."

"Let's get a move on, then."

Chapter Seven

"Yum." Ally breathed in the scent of the gingerbread cookies cooking in the oven in the other room. "I think those smell like they're almost done. Shall we go and check, Fatima?"

The young girl bounded off the chesterfield and followed Ally into the kitchen. Carefully, she opened the oven door so they could peer inside, the heat from the oven warming their cheeks.

"I think they look ready to me." Ally opened the door all the way, put on some oven mitts, and took the hot tray out of the oven, placing it on the stove top.

"They smell so good…" Fatima breathed in the scent of the cookies.

"And I think these ones over here are cooled down enough for us to decorate." Ally gently poked one of the cookies they had made earlier. "Why don't you go and get

Cassie, and then we can start icing them?"

Fatima skipped out of the room. "Cassie! Ally says it's time to decorate the cookies!" Ally smiled at the girl's enthusiasm and began bringing down the ingredients for icing and decorating the cookies.

"It smells like Christmas in here!" Cassie exclaimed, coming into the kitchen a moment later. "Ok, where do we start?"

"How about you get the candy for decorating, and Fatima and I'll start mixing the icing?" The three of them went about their work, humming Christmas carols playing on the radio. A couple of hours later, they had several dozen cookies iced and decorated.

"And now we get to eat them all!"

Ally grinned at Fatima. "Here, why don't you have a couple of these?" She pushed a plate of the test cookies towards her, and Fatima happily tucking into them.

"Just don't eat too many of them or you won't want supper, and Chase will kill me," Ally warned.

"Nah, he likes you too much," Fatima replied confidently.

"Oh, does he now?" Cassie asked, leaning her elbows on the counter, suddenly very attentive to what Fatima was saying. "Tell me more." Ally rolled her eyes at her younger sister, but she found her cheeks going red at the thought that Chase might still have feelings for her. Despite herself, she wanted to hear more of what Fatima had to say, too.

"Mmhmm." Fatima nodded, taking a bite out of a gingerbread woman's arm. "He told me so the other day."

"What exactly did he say?" Ally couldn't stop herself from asking the question.

Fatima shrugged. "He told me how you two used to date in high school, and I asked if he still liked you, and

Yours for the Holiday

he said yes."

Ally took a moment to process this bit of information. Part of her was thrilled to hear that Chase was willing to admit that he still had feelings for her, but part of her was also kind of scared by the thought, especially when she didn't yet know exactly how she felt about him. Ally glanced up and noticed Cassie smirking at her.

"Oh, stop," she chided her.

"I didn't say anything." Cassie held her hands up as if to surrender. "She's the one who said it."

"Yeah, but you were thinking it." Cassie shrugged, the grin on her face getting bigger as she took delight in watching her older sister squirm. The moment was broken when they heard the front door open. Ally revelled in the excuse to get away from her sister's direct gaze and headed out into the hallway, but her joy was short-lived when she saw who it was.

"Wow! It's really coming down out there." Chase hurried inside, a blast of cold air following him in. Ally shivered a bit at the change in temperature. Chase brushed off the heavy snow that coated his hair and clothes. Somehow, he seemed to be even more handsome than ever.

"I had no idea it was supposed to be that bad out," Ally said, looking through the floor-to-ceiling rectangular windows on either side of her parents' front doors. She could barely see a foot into the thick snow coming down.

"It's a full-on blizzard out there." As if Mother Nature wanted to emphasize Chase's point, Ally heard the little *pings!* of freezing rain hitting the windowpanes as the wind picked up.

"So, how's the baking going?" he asked, the happy grin on his face getting brighter as he smelled the gingerbread. "It definitely smells good. Glad to see you haven't burned down the kitchen." His grin returned as he teased her.

"Ha, ha," she replied sarcastically. "I only tried to burn the kitchen down once, and that was when I was fifteen years old. And it's not like I meant to forget the cookies in the oven. In fact, as I seem to remember a certain someone was busy trying to distract me." She arched an eyebrow at him. The two of them had been making out on the couch in the living room when the smoke alarm had gone off. The kitchen had only filled with smoke, and nothing but the cookies had been ruined, but Chase still wouldn't let her forget the incident.

He ran his fingers through his dark hair and chuckled, a sheepish look on his face. "That was a good time." She smiled at him.

"Is Fatima ready?" he asked, changing the subject.

"Yeah, she's just back in the kitchen. I'll go and get her." Just as Ally turned around to head back to the kitchen, the power in the whole house flickered and went out. She heard a little squeal of shock coming from the kitchen, probably from Cassie, who'd never liked the dark.

"Al? Are you there?" she called out from the kitchen.

"Yeah, I'm here." It took a second for her eyes to adjust to the dimness, barely making out Chase's shadowy figure in front of her.

"Here, I have a flashlight." Ally jumped a bit at seeing his face suddenly light up right in front of her, illuminated by the flashlight app on his phone. "Here, I've got another one on my key chain."

She reached out, her hand briefly connecting with his as she took the mini flashlight and flicked it on. The small LED light gave off an eerie blue glow.

"Do your parents still keep the candles and spare flashlights in the cupboard under the stairs?"

Yours for the Holiday

She thought about it for a moment and realized she didn't know the answer. "Uh, I think so… Cassie?"

"What?" her sister yelled back.

"Do Mom and Dad still keep the spare candles under the stairs?"

"Yep!"

"Thanks!" Chase and Ally opened the cupboard, located the candles, and made their way back to the kitchen.

"Chase!" Fatima greeted him. She ran over to him and threw her arms around his waist.

"Hey there, kiddo. You alright?"

"Yeah, I'm not scared." Fatima looked up at him, confident.

"Of course, not. You're the bravest person I know." Ally was touched watching the exchange between them.

"Ally, would you get that out of my face, please?" Cassie asked her, squinting and sounding annoyed. She hadn't realized that while she'd been watching Chase and Fatima, she'd been pointing her flashlight directly at her little sister. Ally teased her by waving the light around her face for a second before lowering it again. Cassie stuck her tongue out at her.

"While you two were finding the candles, I found this." Cassie handed Ally the barbecue starter.

"Well, I guess we could get a fire going?" she suggested. They headed into the living room, Cassie settling herself on the loveseat near the window and Fatima taking the armchair by the fireplace. Ally went around, replacing any empty candleholders, and lit them up.

"Let there be light!" Cassie intoned playfully.

Ally smiled at her and settled herself on the chesterfield with a blanket on her lap, watching Chase as he blew on the embers he'd lit, coaxing them into a little fire. Proud of himself, he rubbed his hands together, warming them.

"That's better, now, isn't it?" He looked at her, a big grin on his face, and she found herself smiling back at him.

"Thanks, Chase."

"May I join you?" he asked, taking the seat beside her.

Ally lifted the blanket. The two of them were sitting so close together that her entire left side was pressed up against him. She immediately felt warmer with him by her side, and it wasn't just from his body warmth or the heat from the fire. It was the sense of comfort and familiarity from being in such close proximity to someone she'd known for so long that warmed her from the inside out. It had been a long time since the two of them had sat together like this. She felt a sense of peace.

A hush descended upon the room. The only sound was the occasional *pop!* of the logs in the fireplace and the pinging of the ice pellets against the window. The snow was still coming down so hard outside that you couldn't see your hand in front of your face, let alone the other brick houses on the other side of the street.

"I hope Mom and Dad are safe out there. If Chase had a hard time walking over here from just next door, I don't want to think about what the roads must be like." Her parents should've been coming home by now, and a sense of worry settled into the pit of her stomach at the thought of them trying to drive home in this weather.

"I'm sure they're fine." Ally felt Chase's strong hand take hers under the blanket, giving it a gentle squeeze of reassurance.

"They texted just before the power went out to say

that they were getting a room at the hotel for the night. They didn't want to try to cross the bridge in this," Cassie confirmed.

"Thank God for that." Ally breathed a sigh of relief.

"See? Nothing to worry about," Chase said quietly, giving her a small smile.

"Speaking of parents, shouldn't you call yours to let them know you made it over here safe and sound? You don't want them to think you got lost in a snowdrift in the driveway."

"I already texted Mom to let her know that Fatima and I would be staying over here until the storm passes, if that's ok with you?"

"Of course. You're always welcome here." She smiled at him.

"I'm hungry," Fatima interrupted the moment.

"Well, I think we can solve that. We have all those cookies we just baked, after all."

"We can't eat cookies for supper, Cass," Ally admonished, noticing the look of disappointment on Fatima's face. "There's still that chicken Mom cut up and left for us in the fridge. I'll go and see what I can scrounge up for us."

"I'll come with you." Chase rose from the chesterfield and followed her into the kitchen, carrying one of the flashlights to light their way.

"Mind shining that over here?" she asked when they were in the kitchen, opening up the fridge door. He came over to stand behind her, close enough for her to feel his warm breath on the back of her neck. A shiver ran through her, and it wasn't from the cool air of the kitchen. She tried to turn her attention back to the contents of the fridge.

"Ok, we have chicken." She pulled out the plate her mother had prepared. "We also have some cranberry sauce and butter, and I think there's some homemade bread over there." She pointed in the direction of one of the countertops.

Chase shone the light in the direction she pointed to. "Yup. I see some over there."

"We also have cold mashed potatoes and squash," she said, pulling out those containers too.

"Alright, let's do up some plates." Chase helped her bring down some of the formica plates from the cupboard and they divvied up the leftovers into four, even portions.

"I miss this," Ally admitted, surprising herself.

Chase paused briefly, a spoonful of squash suspended above the plate. "Yeah?"

"Yeah. I always liked seeing you move around a kitchen. You were always at your most confident when you were in a kitchen." Chase went quiet, something in his posture both pleased at the compliment and curiously sad at the same time.

"Sorry, I shouldn't have brought it up." After their discussion before on the topic, she should've just left the subject of him and cooking, and his dream of opening up his own restaurant alone.

"No, it's ok. I know you were just trying to be supportive before. I'm sorry I snapped at you. It's just…"

"Things are different now? We're different now."

"Yeah. Well, you're surprisingly still the same stubborn Ally I remember," he teased.

"Oh, really? That's how you want to play this, Carter? Because it seems to me like you're definitely the one of us who's stubborn, and that definitely hasn't changed since the last time I saw you."

Yours for the Holiday

Chase gave her a look of feigned shock. "What, me? No way. You're definitely more stubborn than I am."

"Right. So, that's why you're working so hard to win this argument about who's more stubborn?"

"I see your point," he conceded.

"I hear a lot of laughing in there, but I don't see a whole lot of food coming our way!" Cassie shouted from the living room.

"My little sister, folks," Ally joked. "Never one to let a little patience come between her and her stomach."

"Here, let me get those." Chase took two of the plates. "We better get some food into your sister before she turns into a hangry monster and eats us."

She watched him walk out of the kitchen carrying the plates with the confidence of someone who'd been working in a kitchen their whole life. Putting the empty food containers in the sink, she picked up the last two plates and followed him into the living room.

"Here you go." Chase handed Cassie and Fatima each their own plate. He turned around just in time to see Ally carrying in the others.

"Here, I'll hold these while you sit on the couch."

"Thanks." Ally relinquished her plates to him and settled herself under the blanket once more.

"There you go." Chase gave her back her plate and sat down beside her. The four of them set about eating their cold supper in silence. Safe and warm inside, the heavy snow outside had an almost magical, ethereal look. As the thick snowflakes swirled around in the orange glow of the streetlights, it was almost possible to forget that it was a blizzard outside.

"I think this is quite possibly the best dinner I've had in a very long time," Ally exclaimed after a few minutes.

"What about eating out at all those fancy restaurants in L.A.?" Cassie asked her.

"L.A. may have some world-class restaurants, but there's nothing like a home-cooked meal, in candlelight no less."

"Aww… you're so sugary sweet," Cassie teased her. "Speaking of sugar, now can we have some cookies? Please?" Cassie asked her, sounding like she was five years old again.

"Can we?" Fatima chorused with her.

"Did you two eat up all your vegetables?" Ally teased them, sounding mockingly parental. They both nodded.

"Well, then, I suppose."

"Yes!" Fatima exclaimed, victorious.

"How about I bring out one of the pots, and then we can melt down some chocolate and milk, and make hot chocolate over the fireplace?" Chase suggested.

"Yum!" Fatima's face lit up with excitement.

"Care to join me?" Chase rose from the chesterfield, holding out a hand to Ally.

"Sure." She took his hand, feeling its strength in her own. When he released her hand to gather up everyone's plates, she felt a sense of reluctance to let him go. The longer she was home, the more she realized just how much she'd missed him.

"You can put those in the sink, and we'll deal with them tomorrow when the power comes back on," she told him as they entered the kitchen.

"What are you looking for?" Chase asked her, as he brought down some baking chocolate, marshmallows, and five mugs.

"Ouch!" The sound of his voice had startled her as she'd knelt down to look in one of the cupboards in the

Yours for the Holiday

kitchen island, causing her to bang her head.

"I'm looking for a pot to make some hot chocolate…" she mumbled, slowly backing out on all fours, one hand clutching the little key chain flashlight he had given her earlier, the other clutching her head.

"Gah! Owww…" she whined, this time hitting her ankle on the corner of the cupboard behind her.

"Here, let me help you up." Chase came around the island and held out his hand to her again. She wanted to protest, being an independent woman and all, but she also knew that at the rate she was going, she would probably break an arm next.

"Thanks." He clutched her hand firmly and helped her to her feet.

"Now, let me take a look at that." He gently turned her around, taking out his cellphone, careful to shine the light of the phone's flashlight app near her face. Gently, he examined the spot where she'd bumped her head.

"I'm fine, honestly."

"I just want to make sure you didn't cut yourself or something." His fingers were soft as he gently pushed her hair aside and examined her. "It doesn't look too bad. You'll probably have a bump and a sore head in the morning, but nothing a little aspirin can't fix." He let her hair fall gently back into place.

"I'll take a look at that ankle when we're back in the living room. Here, let's get you some ice for it." He turned around towards the fridge and brought down an ice pack from the freezer. "It should still be cold enough to bring down any swelling." He tossed her the ice pack, then opened the fridge and brought out a bag of milk.

"I'm sure I'll be fine. It was just a bump," she said.

"Well, better to be safe than sorry. And the pots are under the stove, now." He reached down, opened up the compartment, and pulled one out.

Ally was surprised by how well he knew her parents' house. It made her feel a little sad, knowing that he knew the place better than she did, even though she was the one who'd grown up here. She hadn't realized being away the last six years, just how much things had changed and moved on without her. Her friends, her family, her childhood home were all still relatively the same as before, but it was the little things, like her mother moving where she kept her pots and pans, that were just enough to make Ally feel like she was a bit of an outsider in her own home.

"What's taking so long in there?" Cassie yelled from the living room. "You two better not be making out in the dark."

Ally burst out laughing. "Yeah, like that'd happen."

She'd said it more out of embarrassment because of the feelings that she'd always had for him that had never quite gone away, no matter how much distance she'd put between them. When she saw his face, she regretted her embarrassment. She couldn't quite make out the expression he made in the dark, but she felt that she'd somehow hurt him, and she felt sorry for it. For the first time since she'd come home, she wondered if maybe he was starting to feel what she was feeling too, and that her trying to deny her own feelings had caused him pain. She was just about to bridge the emotional gap when Chase took an unconscious step back from her.

"Well, looks like we have everything we came for. We should get back." Ally nodded, accepting that he wasn't ready to talk about it yet. Chase gathered everything up, putting it in the pot so it would be easier to carry.

"You got the cookies?"

"Yeah, I'll bring them in." She grabbed one of the containers of gingerbread men from the countertop and

Yours for the Holiday

followed him slowly back to the living room. She tried not to limp, even though her ankle throbbed.

"There you two are!" Cassie explained. "What did you do to your ankle?" Her tone turned from playful teasing to something more serious when she noticed her sister's limp.

"I banged it on the corner of the island when I was looking for a pot."

"What were you doing over by the island? The pots are under the stove," Cassie replied matter-of-factly.

"Yeah, well, I've learned that *now*," Ally snapped back, her tone a little sharper than she'd intended. Her ankle was full on throbbing now, and it was making her cranky. "They were always in the cupboard by the fridge. When did that change?"

"Mom decided to re-organize a couple of years ago." Ally settled herself onto the chesterfield, carefully navigating her sore ankle so that it would be propped up by one of the cushions.

Chase set the pot with the ingredients by the fireplace, then turned his attention to her. "Let's take a look at that ankle now." His fingers gently probed her ankle, and she tried not to wince, trying not to seem like she was in as much pain as she really was.

"That hurts?" Chase asked her, feeling her pain.

"A little," she said, a part of her pleased he was still so in tune with her that he could feel what she was feeling without even having to look at her.

"Well, good news: I don't think it's sprained or broken."

"Told you," she teased, but it was without malice or haughtiness. She let him re-position her leg, so it was supported by the back of the chesterfield and wrapped the ice pack around it.

"Well, how about I get that hot chocolate started?" he asked the room, turning his attention away from her.

"Yes!" Fatima squealed with delight. "And cookies too?"

"And cookies too," he smiled at her, taking the container from Ally and handing it to her.

"You need to share those with everyone," he reminded her.

"Fiiiine." Fatima playfully stuck her tongue out at him before taking out a couple of cookies for herself and handing the container over to Cassie. At the same time, Chase put the pot into the fire, which was slowly burning itself down to embers. He added in the baking chocolate and milk, steadily stirring it carefully so it wouldn't stick to the bottom of the pot.

"Ok, who's ready for some hot chocolate?"

"Me!" Ally, Fatima, and Cassie all chimed in at the same time. As Ally took the blanket off her lap, Chase held up his hand.

"You wait right there, and I'll bring one over to you. You're supposed to be resting that ankle."

Ally scoffed at his over-protectiveness, but secretly, she was glad for it. With Ally no longer in the running for the first mug of hot chocolate, Fatima leapt out of her chair just before Cassie could get to Chase.

"I beat you!" Cassie looked slightly put out.

"Oh, stop," Ally gently chided her. "She's ten years old. Let her have the win."

"Fine," Cassie snarked. She and Fatima collected their mugs, opening the bag of marshmallows and filling their cups.

"Not too many!" Chase warned Fatima.

"Sorry," she grinned, a slick of froth covering her top lip.

Yours for the Holiday

"I think I better take custody of these, or there'll been none left for us," Chase said, dropping a few into his and Ally's mugs, and then walked over to the chesterfield

"And here you go." He gently lifted her legs and sat down beside her, repositioning her legs so that they went over his lap. Reaching over, he picked up their mugs and handed one to her, their fingers brushing ever so slightly.

"Thanks." As Ally sipped away at the warm drink, her tastebuds exploded with the taste of the hot chocolate and marshmallows, and just the tiniest hint of a spice she couldn't quite identify.

"Cinnamon and maple syrup!" she exclaimed.

"What?" Chase gave her a quizzical look.

"Oh, sorry. I did not mean to say that out loud. I was just sitting here drinking this and thinking back to how it tasted exactly like your grandmother's recipe, and I was trying to think of what the secret ingredients were, and then I remembered how we finally, after years of asking, got her to tell us it was cinnamon and hint of maple syrup."

Chase grinned at her. "I didn't think you'd remember that."

"Of course! Sitting in your kitchen on those freezing cold January days in the dead of winter, drinking the hot chocolate your grandmother made us, listening to her as she told us the traditional Mi'kmaq stories her grandmother used to tell her... Those are some of my favourite childhood memories."

Chase placed a hand gently on her shin, and Ally found that she really wanted nothing more in that moment than to lean over and kiss him. Reminding her they weren't alone, Cassie loudly popped the top off the plastic container holding the gingerbread cookies.

"Cookie anyone?" she asked in a voice far louder

than was necessary, and gave Ally a pointed look. Ally shrugged and mouthed "What?" with Cassie rolling her eyes at her in response.

"I'll take one or three!" Fatima giggled.

"Two, at most," Chase admonished her. "It's going to be bed-time soon enough and the last thing we all need is you being wound up on a sugar high all night."

"Hey, can we play a game?" Fatima asked, changing the topic while sneaking another cookie onto her plate. Chase gave her a look to let her know that he'd seen what she'd done, but didn't say anything further.

"I think we have some board games somewhere, don't we, Cass?"

"Yeah, we keep them under the stairs." Cassie pointed vaguely in the direction of the staircase. "We have Scrabble, Monopoly, and Clue. I'd have to get up and see if we have anything else. Does anyone have a preference?"

Fatima paused to think about it for a second. "Let's play Monopoly!"

"Monopoly it is!" Cassie got up from the loveseat and brought the game out of the cupboard while Fatima cleared some space off the coffee table.

"Did no one just hear me say that it's almost bed-time?" Chase asked.

"Oh yeah, we heard you. We just decided to ignore you." Ally grinned wickedly at him.

"I call the top hat!" Fatima declared, snatching it up before the others could take it.

"Alright then," Ally laughed, carefully leaning over to take the thimble as Cassie claimed the shoe. Ally picked up the iron and held it out to Chase. "You in?"

"I guess so. Let's play, but don't be sore losers when I beat you all."

"Oh, ho! We'll see about that," Ally replied,

Yours for the Holiday

suddenly feeling very competitive as she picked up the dice to roll for her turn.

A few hours later, somewhere near midnight, no matter how hard Fatima tried to keep their spirited game going, they were all yawning.

"Alrighty, time for bed," Chase said. There were some protests from Cassie and Fatima, but both were barely holding their eyes open.

"Fine. As long as you all admit that I clearly won this round," Cassie said.

Ally eyed the huge stacks of paper money on her side of the table. "I don't think that anyone's going to dispute that. I think you've got all our money, and then some," she teased. Cassie let out an enormous yawn, grinning in victory like the Cheshire cat.

Chase carefully lifted Ally's legs from his lap and stood up. Fatima had nodded off in her chair. Looking out the window at the snow still coming down, she turned to Chase. "Why don't you and Fatima take Mom and Dad's room?"

"Thanks." Chase quietly moved to Fatima's side and gently picked her up and moved towards the stairs.

"Here, wait a second." Ally hobbled around the room, blowing out the candles. "Don't want to burn the place down while we're asleep." She grabbed her cell phone and turned on the flashlight app before blowing out the last candle, leaving the fire – which had burned down to the embers – to put itself out. "I'll light your way up."

She followed slowly behind him, shining the light just over his shoulder so they wouldn't trip going upstairs.

"My parents' room is just over there," she said, pointing out the master bedroom opposite to her and Cassie's rooms.

"I remember," he said, smiling. "I particularly

remember trying to avoid getting caught sneaking past it after our midnight curfew." Ally laughed quietly, careful not to wake up Cassie, whom she could hear snoring gently in the next room.

"It's always amazed me that my parents planned on putting mine and Cassie's rooms opposite theirs so they could hear anyone coming and going from our bedrooms at night, but they totally forgot about the trellis right outside my window."

"Maybe they thought no one would be crazy enough to climb down that rickety old thing."

"Oh, so you admit you're crazy, then?" she teased him, bringing up memories of when he would sneak in and out of her room.

Chase chuckled. "Good night, Ally. Thanks for everything. It's been the most fun I've had in a very long time."

"Me too."

She watched as he walked into her parents' bedroom and gently laid Fatima down on the bed before turning towards her own bedroom.

"Goodnight, Chase."

Chapter Eight

    Ally woke in the grey of the early morning light to the sound of a snow-plow clearing the street. She rubbed blearily at her eyes, staring up at her ceiling for a moment, adjusting herself to her surroundings. The house was still and quiet. She turned over onto her side, noticing that the light of her alarm clock was blinking. The power had come back on sometime while they'd slept.

    She reluctantly rose from her bed, padding quietly across the hall towards the bathroom. On the way, she quietly peered into her parents' room. She smiled to see Fatima asleep on the bed while Chase slept in the armchair near the window, the quilt he'd wrapped around himself having slipped down to his lap sometime in the night, exposing the upper part of his body to the cold air. Ally quietly moved over to his side and paused a moment to watch him as he slept. His face seemed so peaceful, all the cares and worries of the world erased in his slumber. Ally bent down and adjusted the quilt, tucking it in around his shoulders. Chase stirred at her touch, a smile coming over his face as his eyes recognized her.

"Good morning," he whispered. His voice was low and thick with sleep.

"Good morning."

"How's your ankle?" He looked down at her foot, apparently noticing that she seemed to be standing on it just fine.

"It twinges a bit, but doesn't really hurt. Must have been all that TLC you gave me last night."

He smiled at her. "Is the power back on?"

"Yeah. It must've come on sometime after we went to bed."

Something in his expression seemed almost disappointed that their magical time together last night was coming to an end. Chase glanced over at the bed, seeing that Fatima was still asleep. "I suppose I should get her up and we should make our way back over to my parents' place."

It was Ally's turn to look disappointed. "Or you could both stay for breakfast," she suggested, giving a little shrug, as if it didn't really matter to her either way.

"Is that your way of asking if I'll stay long enough to make you breakfast?" he asked, a cheeky grin on his face.

Ally gave him a look of mock surprise. "What, me? I'd never suggest you stay for breakfast just so that I could have you make it for me. I don't know what you're talking about."

"Yes, you would." He smirked at her, the both of them knowing that he was right.

"Fine. I might have selfish reasons for wanting you to stay, but maybe I just also happen to want you to stay a bit longer."

Yours for the Holiday

Chase stared into her eyes for a second, taking in what she had said. He didn't have the chance to respond, though, because they both heard Fatima stir on the bed next to them. Chase rose from the chair and came over to the bed.

"Well, good morning, sleepy head."

"Morning," Fatima said sleepily, rubbing her eyes. She looked around the room, her eyes landing on Ally. "Hi!"

"Good morning to you, too," Ally smiled at her. "Are you hungry?"

"Starving!"

"Well, it's a good thing Chase offered to make us some breakfast then, isn't it?" Ally gave him a pointed look.

He put his hands up in a gesture of defeat. "Well, I guess I better get downstairs and get started on breakfast."

"Thanks Chase." Ally smiled at him as he moved past her towards the kitchen. When he'd left the room, Ally turned to Fatima.

"If you need to go to the bathroom or anything, you'd better do it now before Cassie gets up, because once she does, she'll be in there forever."

"Okay." Fatima rose from the bed and headed out towards the upstairs bathroom. Ten minutes later, Ally and Fatima were both ready for the day, and the scent of whatever delicious meal Chase was making was wafting its way up the stairs. Ally headed over to her sister's room and quietly knocked on the door.

"Cass? Time to get up. Chase is making us breakfast." Cassie mumbled something incoherently.

"Cass! Time to get up!" Ally repeated herself, more loudly this time.

"Wha-?" She sat up straight in bed, peering at Ally through sleepy eyes.

"Breakfast. Downstairs. Now."

"Oh, ok. Does that mean we have power again?" Ally reached into her sister's room and flipped on the light switch, flooding the room with light.

"What the - ?!"

"Hey! Watch what you say next," Ally cut her off, nodding toward Fatima, who was standing right beside her.

"What the h-e-double-hockey-sticks did you do that for?" Cassie asked, her sleep-addled brain registering what her older sister was getting at.

"You two know that I'm ten, not five, right? I do know what that spells."

Ally chuckled. "Well, she still shouldn't be saying it in front of you. Come on, everyone. Breakfast smells like it's almost ready."

The three of them headed downstairs to where Chase was standing in front of the stove, a whole feast of fresh fruit, eggs, pancakes, and toast laid out for them.

"You're just in time." Chase turned around at their arrival, putting scrambled eggs on each of the four plates he'd laid out on the kitchen island. Ally and the others slid onto the stools, tucking into their breakfast.

After they had finished their meals, Chase turned to Fatima and said, "Well, kiddo. I think it's time that we head home now."

"Nooo… Do we have to?" Fatima stuck her bottom lip out, giving Chase her best puppy dog eyes.

"Yes, it's definitely time for you to go home, and I have to go to work today and check on the residents, and we still have that dance to plan. Christmas Eve is just around the corner." Fatima pouted, but seemed to accept Chase's decision.

"Now, let's say thank you to Ally and Cassie for letting us stay over, and we'll clean up these dishes, and then we'll be on our way."

"Thank you for letting us stay over last night. I had the best time!"

"You are very welcome! We loved having you both." Ally smiled at both her and Chase. "And don't worry about the dishes. I couldn't let you clean them up after making you stay and cook us breakfast. We'll clean up."

"You sure? I don't mind." Despite Chase's earlier words about wanting to head across the driveway to his parents' place, Ally had the feeling that there was a part of him that wanted to find any excuse to linger just a little longer.

"No, it's fine. We've got them covered. You two should head on home and check in with your parents."

"Well, alright then. Thanks for everything." He surprised her by reaching over and giving her a hug. It felt incredible having his arms around her like this that she found herself holding him a bit longer than was absolutely necessary.

Chase cleared his throat.

"Well, I guess I'll see you later today to help decorate the rest of the rec room?" she asked.

"Yeah, that'd be great. Did you want me to drive you over?"

"Sure. Yeah, just give me like an hour to shower and such and I'll be ready to go."

"An hour? You mean more like two, right?" he teased her. Ally playfully punched him in the arm.

"Hey! That was uncalled for."

"It was totally called for! You can't just insult a lady by saying that she takes too long in the bathroom and then not expect to get hit in return. It takes a lot of time and primping to go from this," she motioned towards her pajama-clad, make-up free appearance, "To the version of me that looks halfway presentable for the rest of the world."

"You don't need all that stuff to make you look beautiful." Ally was stunned by his comment, momentarily shocked into silence.

"So, you said you wanted to get on your way?" Cassie asked, interrupting the moment. Ally shot her sister a quizzical look.

"Yeah, that's right. Fatima, let's get your boots and coat on."

When they were safely out of earshot, Ally turned to Cassie. "What was that all about?" she hissed.

"I don't know what you're talking about." Cassie shrugged her shoulders, feigning ignorance, but Ally knew her too well to know that this was far from the truth.

"The whole time I've been home, you've been pushing me to get together with Chase, and now suddenly you've changed your mind?"

"I do!" Cassie looked sheepishly at her, like she knew she'd done something wrong, but there was also something in her eyes that was curiously defiant as well.

"Oh, really? So, what was with you acting weird every time Chase and I got close last night?"

"Well…"

"What?" Ally pressed.

"I just didn't think it was good for Fatima to see you two getting so close," she finally admitted. "It's one thing for the two of you to be all flirty and sexy with each other when it's just the two of you, but you're only here for a few more days, and I just don't want to see you two get into something where one or both of you are going to get your hearts broken, or worse, get Fatima's hopes up. You may get to go back to L.A. soon, but I have to stay here and watch Chase try to put his life together again if you end up breaking his heart, just like…"

"Like the last time," she finished her sentence. She knew Cassie was right, despite how good it felt being around Chase again.

"You don't know what those two have been through since you were away, and it wouldn't just be Chase's heart you'd break this time, but Fatima's, too."

"Ok, so tell me, then." Ally hadn't forgotten about their conversation from the other day.

"I think Mom's right. I think that's better coming from Chase."

Ally sighed, frustrated. What was it that was so bad that no one could bring themselves to tell her about it?

"Besides, I kinda like having my big sister around and I don't want you to skip off back to L.A. and then not come home again for another six years because you're afraid to face Chase Cormier." Cassie nervously fidgeted with a strand of her blonde hair.

"Oh Cass." Ally was shocked to hear that her sister thought that Chase had been why she hadn't come home in so long. "You know that me being out in L.A. has nothing to do with Chase, right?"

"Obviously not, or I wouldn't have brought it up."

"Well, he's not the reason I'm out there. It's just… I went from being someone here who had the potential to go somewhere and do great things, and shine really bright, and then I went out to L.A. and found thousands of other people just like me and then suddenly I realized that I wasn't the shiniest star that I thought I was. I stayed out in L.A. all this time because I didn't want to come home a failure. I wanted to make something of myself before I faced you all again."

"You know we all love you no matter if you're

some big Hollywood star or if you're doing something else that's just as awesome. I know I don't say this very often, but you're kind of my hero." Cassie came around the kitchen island and gave her a big hug.

"Do you mean that?"

"Of course! How many other people have the guts you do to go out there and follow their dreams like that?"

Ally wrapped her sister in a tight hug. "I love you, sis."

"Love you, too."

"Can we get in on these hugs too?" The two of them looked up at their parents, who were standing in the doorway.

"Mom! Dad! So glad you made it home safe." Cassie ran over to her parents, giving them the big hug they'd asked for.

"That was quite some storm, wasn't it?" their dad said, hugging her back.

"Yeah, it was."

"We just bumped into Chase on the way in, just now. He said that he and Fatima slept over last night?" Ally's mother directed this question to her, giving her a sly smile. "What did the four of you get up to?"

Ally nibbled her bottom lip, suddenly embarrassed at having everyone's attention on her and Chase once more. "Oh, you know, the usual. Board games and sitting around the fireplace. Nothing much."

"Uh huh," her mother responded, sounding slightly skeptical. "Well, why don't I put on a pot of tea, and you can tell me all about it?"

༄༅༅

Yours for the Holiday

"And where are you heading off too?" Ally's mother asked, coming over to the staircase where Ally was putting on her boots an hour later.

"I told Chase I would go in with him to the nursing home and finish the decorating for the dance today."

Her mother nodded. "You two seem to be spending quite a lot of time together since you got home. Just like old times. You two were always inseparable."

"Yeah, well, you know; Grams kind of volunteered me to help him with the dance, and I don't want to let her down." Ally shrugged, but even she knew she wasn't being that convincing. "If you want to ask me if Chase and I are getting back together, Mom, just ask. Stop beating around the bush."

"Ok. Are you and Chase back together?"

Ally paused briefly while zipping up her jacket. "No, Mom, we're not."

"But things might move in that direction?"

Ally glanced down at her boots, knowing that if she stared her mother directly in the eyes that her expression would betray her. "No, Mom. You don't have anything to worry about. Chase and I are not getting back together."

Ally couldn't help but feel a bit hurt when her mother breathed a sigh of relief. "I know that your sister and I have teased you a bit about the two of you working on this dance together since you came home, but if I'm being honest, I'm a bit relieved to hear you say that."

"You don't say," Ally muttered under her breath.

Her mother ignored the comment, but Ally knew she had heard it all the same. "It's not that I don't like Chase…"

"You just don't want to see me hurt him again? Yeah, there's a lot of that going around today." Ally felt resentment and annoyance rising inside her.

"It wasn't easy for me to leave him like that, you know. It's not like he was the only one who got hurt. Just because I wasn't here for you to see it every day doesn't mean that there weren't plenty of times that I felt like crying on the kitchen floor about it." Ally knew she was being petty, but she had the feeling that everyone in her family was ganging up on her and she wasn't much in the mood to stand for it. She was relieved when she heard Chase's truck starting next door.

"That's Chase. I've got to go. See you later, Mom."

Chapter Nine

"Brrr..." Fatima rubbed her mittened hands together, furiously trying to warm them. Chase reached over and turned the fan up all the way, even though the truck's heating system hadn't warmed up yet and was mostly just blowing around more cold air. Wanting to get moving, Chase gave two quick, sharp blasts on the truck's horn to let Ally know they were ready to go.

"Where is she?" he muttered under his breath. No sooner than he'd uttered the words and the Hayes' front door opened, and she emerged.

"Hi Ally!" Fatima called through the window, waving enthusiastically at her. Although Ally waved back, there was something about the stiffness of her posture, the tightness of her smile that told him that something had happened in the hour since he'd left her place.

"Hey there," Chase greeted her as she opened the

door and climbed into the truck.

"Hey." A long pause fell between the two of them.

"Is something wrong?" he finally asked.

"No."

Chase nodded silently and put the truck in drive. He knew she wasn't telling him the truth, but he also knew her well enough to know that he just needed to leave her alone for a bit, and she'd let him know when she was ready. Fatima, for her part, didn't seem to notice the silence and was more than happy to fill it with her own chatter until they arrived at the nursing home.

"So, what are we going to work on today?" Fatima asked Ally, skipping inside the nursing home.

"I thought we could decorate the tree." Ally's mood seemed to have improved the longer she was around Fatima. Her infectious enthusiasm was difficult to ignore.

"That sounds like fun! I'm going to go and find the boxes where we keep the ornaments."

"Go and ask Josh for help in getting them down." Fatima skipped down the hall towards Josh's office.

"I should help her," Chase said to Ally, rethinking his decision. "I'll meet you in the rec room?"

"See you in a few." She smiled at him, and he felt better now that she seemed to have put whatever it was this morning behind her. Chase went to the end of the hallway to help Josh bring down the paltry amount of decorations they had for the tree.

"This is it?" he asked.

"Yeah, sorry. Not much room in the budget for decorations. Most of this has been donated or left over from residents who are no longer with us."

"Well, I guess we'll make do with what we've got."

"I bet Ally can do something spectacular with it," Fatima replied confidently.

Yours for the Holiday

"What's this?" Ally asked, overhearing some of their conversation as they entered the rec room.

"Fatima here was just instilling us with lots of confidence in your abilities to fairy godmother this place out of these few boxes of mismatched decorations." They turned around to watch as Fatima moved around the seniors, chatting away to each of them animatedly.

"She's something special, isn't she?"

"Yeah, she is," he replied proudly. He felt her curiosity and knew what she wanted to ask him, about what happened during those six years she'd been gone. He'd told her some of it, but he knew she craved to know more. He wanted to explain it all to her, but being with her these last few days had reminded him of the person he used to be, the one who could smile and laugh again, and be happy. He knew that telling her about Samar would make her see him differently, and he was more than a little afraid that it would make her run back to L.A. for good this time.

"Where do we start?" Fatima asked, coming back over to them.

"Chase and Josh, why don't you two start with the garland?" Ally handed them the strings of fake garland from the box. "Once they've got that on, we can put on the lights, and then we can put on the ornaments." The entire group set about their work. They'd been working for several minutes when Ally's cellphone rang.

"Sorry, I need to get this." She handed Chase the angel for the top of the tree and pulled out her phone.

"Hello?" She walked a few steps away, her body half-turned away. Chase tried to suss out the nature of the conversation from the micro-expressions on her face, a face that he'd once known as his own. He tried to listen on the conversation while simultaneously pretending to very intent on unravelling a string of lights.

"Ok. Yeah. Thanks for letting me know." She hung up the phone and rejoined the group. "Sorry about that." She stood beside him and grabbed her own batch of lights, trying to disentangle them from one another. Her face and posture were all completely calm, a little too calm for his liking.

"Something wrong?"

"No. No, actually, just the opposite. That was the casting agent for a role I auditioned for before I came out here. I just got the part." Her face lit up as bright as the Christmas tree beside them. "I can't believe it! My luck has *finally* begun to change!"

"That's great news! Congratulations!" He strove to stop his voice from sounding disappointed and gave her a hug. He could feel the excitement radiating from her and he tried his best to put aside his devastation that she'd be leaving again. This was what Josh had feared from the beginning: that he'd get used to Ally being home, only for her to leave again. A quick glance at Josh's face confirmed what he was thinking.

"Thanks! I can't quite believe it. I think I'm in shock."

"So, when do you start?" he asked, pulling back from her a bit.

"Boxing Day. I need to fly out that night and we begin filming the next day."

"Wow, so soon… I guess this means you won't be here for as long as you thought, then." His eyes drifted to the floor, trying to turn his face away from her so she wouldn't see the look on it.

"No, I guess not." He didn't know what to make of her expression as it dimmed a bit at this realization. He didn't want to take away the joy she felt at finally getting a role she was proud of, but he also couldn't help but feel a

Yours for the Holiday

little comforted that she seemed to be as conflicted as him about it, too.

"Wait... you're leaving?" Fatima asked, overhearing their conversation. As much as Chase felt upset at Ally's recent good fortune, it made it all the worse knowing that Fatima was going to take Ally's leaving even harder. She'd become so attached to her in such a short time. It had been amazing, really, how the two of them had bonded. In another lifetime, he would've been thrilled at this, but now, he knew it was only going to lead to heartbreak for all of them.

"Yeah, I need to head out right after Christmas." Ally crouched down a bit to be more at the same level as Fatima. Chase couldn't stop his chest from constricting at the way Fatima's face fell. "But I'll still be here for the dance, at least. And Christmas Day."

Fatima still looked disappointed. Chase couldn't blame her.

"Well, hey now, it's not like Ally's leaving right this second, right? We still have a dance to plan," he said, trying to lighten the mood again. "So, let's spend as much time with her as we can and get this dance together."

Fatima perked up again. "Yeah, you're right. C'mon. We still have a tree to finish decorating. Still want to help me?"

"Of course," Ally smiled as she stood up again.

Chase put on a brave face as he watched the two of them take the string of lights and add them to the tree, the two of them smiling and laughing with each other. He couldn't help but look at the two of them together and not think about how things could have been if the situation was different, but as it was, it was all he could do to stop from kidding himself that the worst was yet to come.

Later that evening, Ally dialled Liv's number. "Liv? Do you have a moment?"

"I always have time for you, Ally." She grinned at her.

"Ok, are you sitting down?"

"I am now." Liv's voice sounded intrigued. "What's up?"

"I got the part!"

"OMG that's amazing news, Ally! I'm so happy for you!"

"Thanks! I'm so excited!" Ally still felt like she was a bit in shock. Then she remembered that her good news wasn't the only news they were waiting to hear back on. "Have you heard anything about the role you went for?"

"Well, it's funny you ask about that, because I did, and I got the part!" They both squealed in delight.

"I'm so excited for this!" Ally exclaimed. "Can you believe it? You and I working on the same film together? It's going to be so awesome."

"I can't wait to get started. I just wish we didn't have to cut our trips short."

"I know what you mean," Ally said, thinking back to the look of disappointment on Chase and Fatima's faces when she'd told them about her getting the part. She'd never been so happy, and yet, so heartbroken all at once before.

"Uh oh. What's that look for? Did your family not take the news about you having to leave early well?"

"No, nothing like that," Ally admitted. "I haven't actually told them yet. My Grams is going to join us for supper tonight, and I thought I'd tell them then. No, I was

Yours for the Holiday

just thinking of Chase and Fatima when I told them. They were there when I got the call, and you should've seen the look of disappointment on Fatima's face. It was heartbreaking."

"You're really getting attached to those two, aren't you?" Liv asked her, a curious look on her face.

"Yeah…" she admitted. "I just can't help it. Fatima's the biggest sweetheart you'll ever meet, and Chase…" There was so much she could say to describe him, and yet all the words in the English language didn't seem enough.

"So, what's new with you? How's your holiday going?" she asked, changing the subject.

"Well, no ring yet," Liv responded, knowing what she was getting at. "But we've had loads of quality time together. Lots of skiing and snuggling up by the fireplace."

"Sounds cozy." Ally smiled.

"It's been so good for us! It's just what we needed. Everything in L.A. is all go, go, go. It's so nice to slow down and spend some quality time together. Speaking of quality time, don't think I didn't notice how you avoided the question earlier. How's your time with a certain Chase Cormier going?"

"I'm not going to lie. It's going to be difficult to leave Fatima behind. She's really grown on me," Ally deflected once more.

"And what about a certain Mr. Cormier? It's not going to be easy to leave him behind either, is it?" Liv asked, not letting the topic go.

Ally rolled her eyes, even though she knew Liv couldn't see her. "What is it with you and Fatima both trying to set Chase and I up? She pretends like she isn't thrilled at seeing the two of us together, but I know she is. I swear the two of you are working together."

"Maybe we just see what you don't," Liv pointed out. "I think it means that you and Chase are meant to be together, and you can't deny that. Fatima sounds like she has good taste. I want to meet this girl one day."

"I think she'd like that. She's fascinated by everything Hollywood right now."

"Ah, to be that age again," Liv said, dreamily. "Oh, well, it looks like that's all the time I've got right now. We've got a dinner date at the ski lodge, and I need to get dressed for it."

"You two have fun!"

"Love you!" Liv waved at her before hanging up.

Ally hung up her phone as she heard her father come through the front door with her grandmother. She got up from her bed and headed downstairs to join her family in the kitchen.

"There you are," her grandmother greeted her.

"Sorry, I was just calling my friend back in L.A. Well, we know each other from L.A. but she's in Vermont right now on a romantic getaway with her boyfriend."

"Speaking of romance, how are things going with the dance?" her grandmother asked, winking at her.

"The rec room is looking good, and the plans for the dance are coming along fine," Ally replied, giving her grandmother a knowing look and pointedly staying off the topic of romance. "I think we'll have everything ready in time."

"That's good to hear," her mother chimed in, joining them in the kitchen.

"Where's Dad?" She was eager to share her news about the role she got, and she wanted her whole family around to tell them at once.

"He's just getting the food from the car. Why?"

"I've got something I want to talk to all four of you

Yours for the Holiday

about."

Her mother, grandmother, and sister all looked at her, suddenly alert and suspicious, like they were bracing for bad news. Just then, they heard her father open the front door, kick the snow off his boots, and the faint rustle of the paper bags with their Chinese takeout.

"Get in here," her mother called out to him. "Ally wants to talk to us."

Ally waited as patiently as she could while her father took off his coat and boots and placed the takeout on the counter, but her excitement bubbled over.

"Oh, Dad! Would you hurry up?" she blurted out impatiently.

"What's the hurry?" he asked, fluffing his hair back into place after taking off his hat.

"Just come over here. I need to tell you all something."

Her father, never one to be rushed into doing anything, reluctantly came over to stand by her mother, an expectant look on his face. That made her father stand at attention. They all seemed to hold their breath in anticipation.

"Well?" Cassie asked, looking at her in anticipation.

"So, I know you're going to be disappointed, and I know this is last minute," she started. "But I got a call from my agent, and I've gotten the supporting role in that upcoming rom-com I was waiting to hear back about!"

"Oh, my!" her mother put her hand to her chest. "That's so wonderful!"

"I knew you could do it!" Cassie said, throwing her arms around her sister. "I'm so proud of you, sis!"

"Thanks for convincing me to hang in there and not call my agent, and totally ruin my shot at this." She gave Cassie a radiant smile.

"I expect a special shout-out in your acceptance speech at the Oscars," Cassie teased, only half-joking.

Ally laughed. "You betcha!"

"I'm so proud of you, my dear." Ally's father came over and planted a big kiss on her cheek. "You deserve this, kiddo."

"When does this movie start shooting?" her mother asked, wiping away some tears of joy with a Kleenex.

"Well, that's the thing. I have to leave on Boxing Day to fly back to L.A. We begin filming the next day."

Her mother seemed disappointed, but still proud of her. "Well, it's not as much time together as we'd hoped, but how can we be upset when it's such a great opportunity for you! Now, tell us all about this role."

"Well, there's not much I *can* tell you," she began. "And not only for legal reasons. I haven't even seen a full script yet, so even I don't know much beyond the description of the role my agent gave me. But I think it's going to be a cute film. I think you're going to like it."

"Of course, we are!" her dad said. "My little girl's going to be in it, so of course we're going to like it."

Ally smiled at them, grateful to have such a loving and supportive family.

"Right, well, if we only have a few days left with you, then we should get started on making this the best Christmas you've ever had. Who knows how long it might be before we see you again? Not that I'm complaining. If it means you're following your dreams, then we'll have Christmas in July for the next few years, if we have to. Or, we could come out to L.A. and visit you now that you're going to be a successful actress."

Ally smiled at how her parents were making such a big deal of this when she was hardly a famous actress.

"Well la-di-da! My sister's a famous actress now!" Cassie poked fun of her, smiling and laughing along with her.

"From your lips to God's ears," Ally laughed along with her.

※

"It sucks that Ally's going back to Hollywood."

"Yeah, it does," Chase agreed as he helped Fatima get into her bed. There was no way to sugarcoat it for her. "But we knew she wasn't going to be staying here long anyways. She's just leaving a few days earlier than she originally planned, and it's for a good reason. I mean, it's great that she's got this part that she was going for, right?"

"Yeah, I suppose," Fatima conceded, leaning back into her pillows.

"So, why such the long face?"

"I like her," Fatima replied. "She's a really nice person."

"Yeah, that she is." Chase couldn't help but smile as he thought of Ally.

"Truth is, I kind of thought you two might get back together." She picked at one of the cuticles on her fingers.

Chase raised his eyebrows. "Oh, really?" His tone dripped with sarcasm. "I never would've guessed."

"Yeah..."

"So, all this about the two of us just having to plan this dance together..." he teased.

"I just thought that it might help get the two of you together again. When Kayla was showing me pictures of you and her together in high school, you seemed so happy. You haven't been that happy in a long time. I just wanted to see you smile again. A real smile," she emphasized. "Like, laugh out loud kind of smile."

Chase inhaled sharply, trying to stop tears forming at the corners of his eyes. "I was happy when Ally and I were together back then," he conceded truthfully. "But that was a long time ago. We're different people now, with different lives and different goals. We aren't those same people anymore."

"I know…" she said, her voice sad. "I know that you still love Mom, and you always will, but I thought the same might be true about Ally. I thought she might still be the right person for you."

Chase smiled as he thought of Samar. He still missed her every single day. Having Ally home hadn't changed that, but she'd made the days a little more bearable since she'd been around. He leaned over and kissed her on the forehead. "I know you want me to be happy, Fatima, but it's my job to be the adult and your job not to worry about things like that. I can take care of myself."

"I know you can, but it doesn't mean you have to. Everyone should have someone who takes care of them. You haven't had someone to take care of you since Mom. I thought Ally could be that person."

"Ok. Well, we can talk about this again sometime when and if there's someone in my life that I think might become a little more permanent," Chase conceded, trying to compromise. After all, her intentions were pure; he couldn't punish her for caring too much.

"Just please promise me you'll consider that person being Ally," Fatima pleaded.

Chase tried not to chuckle at her persistence. "I can't promise that, but I can promise that if that changes, you'll be the first to know."

Fatima thought this over. "Ok…" She held out her

hand for a pinky swear.

"You strike a tough bargain." Chase lifted his pinky. "I pinky swear I won't rule out getting back together with Ally, as long as you don't get your hopes up too high about it."

"Deal."

Chase knew she was totally going to get her hopes up, anyway.

Chapter Ten

Christmas Eve

"What are you planning to wear to the dance?" Cassie asked her, plopping herself onto Ally's bed and looking through her suitcase.

"I was thinking of wearing this." She held up a black lace cocktail dress.

"Wow! That's gorgeous!" Cassie reached out and felt the fabric. "It must have cost a whole month's rent! Is it couture?"

"Yes, it is, and it didn't cost as much as you might think," Ally teased.

"Ugh! Why can't I live in L.A. and have couture outfits? How on earth did you afford it?"

"If you know the right second-hand shops to look in, you can find all sorts of pieces for really reasonable prices."

"This is second-hand?" Cassie asked in a shocked tone. "You'd never be able to tell."

"Probably some actress who wore it to an award show decades ago and didn't want it anymore, so it ended up in a second-hand shop," Ally said, as if it were no big deal. "If you're willing to spend time sifting through hundreds of clothes, you too can dress like an A-lister on a fraction of the budget." Ally gave her best telemarketing impression and giggled.

"Take me back to L.A. with you and teach me your ways," Cassie mockingly begged her.

"Any time you want to visit me in L.A., you've got a place to stay," Ally told her. "I'd love to have you out there with me for a visit. I'll take you to all the best shops."

"If only I could…" Cassie replied, dreamily. "But, alas, I've got university and there's the problem of me not having any money. But now that my sister's a big-time actress, maybe she can pay for me to come out and visit."

"Ha!" Ally exclaimed. "The money I'm getting for this role is going to dig me out of credit card debt so I can afford things like proper groceries again. Besides, I'm already offering to let you stay with me for free and I'm going to loan you a couture dress for the Christmas dance; now you want me to pay for you to come out to L.A., too? You could at least shill out something for this visit."

"I'm gracing you with my presence. That should be payment enough," Cassie teased. "Wait! Did you say that you're going to let me borrow one of your couture dresses?"

"Yes, I did."

"You're the best big sister ever!" Cassie rose from the bed and threw her arms around her neck. Ally hugged her back.

"So, what are you going to accessorize with the

dress?" Cassie asked, her one-track mind back on clothes.

"I'm not sure…" Ally turned to her dresser and opened her old jewellery box. She'd left most of her jewellery behind when she'd gone to L.A., so she had lots of options to look through. She pulled out a set of pearl earrings that her grandmother had given her for her sixteenth birthday.

"How about these?"

"Good choice," Cassie said, looking at the earrings like she was imaging how they'd look with the dress.

Ally turned to put them back when her fingers touched the jewellery box's secret compartment. It was empty now, but it had once contained the charm bracelet Chase had given her for her eighth birthday. She'd lost it one day in high school and been heartbroken ever since. It had once been her favourite piece of jewellery, the one piece she couldn't bear to leave the house without. She'd always thought of it as her lucky bracelet, the talisman she'd clung to for every big moment in her life, hoping it would shift the tides in her favour.

"What are you looking at?"

"Nothing," Ally replied quickly, closing the box. The last thing she needed was Cassie on her case about Chase again.

"Ok, well, I'm going to take this and get ready. Thanks, Al. It's beautiful!" Ally smiled as she watched her sister bounding out of her room like a little kid.

Thirty minutes later, she heard Cassie's voice floating up the stairs. "C'mon, Al! Hurry up!"

"Coming!" she shouted back, applying some more lip gloss and teasing out her curls a bit. She wouldn't admit it to herself or anyone, but she was getting dressed up for Chase, and she wanted to look perfect.

It was tradition for the Hayes, Allaby, and Barrett families to have a Christmas Eve party at the Cormiers'

Yours for the Holiday

house that was open to the whole neighbourhood. The tradition had originally started with the Barretts after Kayla and her mom had moved into their new home across from Ally's house. Her dad had been stationed overseas on his first tour in the Middle East for their first Christmas in their new house, so her mother had held a Christmas Eve party to get to know their neighbours. After Kayla's mom had passed away, Chase's mother had carried on the tradition. Ally's family repaid the favour the next day by inviting the Barretts, Allabys, and Cormiers over to their house for Christmas dinner.

Ally headed downstairs and joined her family. As she climbed the steps to Chase's parents' house a few minutes later, she noticed there were shoes outside by the door with what looked like straw coming out of them.

"What's up with the shoes?" Ally gave Chase a curious look as he opened the door to greet them.

"It's for the camel!" Fatima said before Chase could reply. She'd popped up beside him as soon as she'd heard Ally's voice.

"The camel?" she asked, confused.

"You know, the camel that brought the magi to Bethlehem? It leaves presents for children at Christmas."

"It's kind of like us leaving out stockings for Santa," Chase explained.

"That's cool!"

"Here, let me take that for you." Chase held his arms out to take her coat from her. She turned around, letting him slide it off her shoulders, and she shivered a bit at the change in temperature.

"You look… really nice." Chase gave her an appreciative look, taking in her little black dress.

"Thanks," she replied, suddenly self-conscious, but in a good way. "You don't look so bad yourself." Actually, he looked more than "not bad." He looked gorgeous in his suit and he smelled good too; his cologne wafted her way as he came closer to her.

"C'mon in and let's get you something warm to drink." He hung her coat up in the closet and took her by the hand, leading her through the crowded hallway to the kitchen. In typical Maritime fashion, the whole neighbourhood seemed to be piled into the kitchen.

"Here, this'll warm you up." Chase placed a warm mug in her hands. She breathed in the scent of peppermint hot chocolate, with more than a hint of Baileys in it.

"Mmhmm… this smells lovely." She took a sip, careful not to let it burn her tongue.

"Ally! Want to come and look at all the presents I've got under the tree?" Fatima asked, interrupting the moment between them.

"Fatima, I'm not sure that Ally really needs to see *all* your presents…" Chase began.

"Are you kidding? Of course, I want to see them!" Ally cut in enthusiastically. She let Fatima take her by the hand and lead her back through the crowds to the living room.

"Wow! That's one impressive pile of presents." Ally noticed the colourfully wrapped boxes under the tree. "Are all these for you?"

"No," Fatima replied, her tone implying she knew that Ally already knew this. "But this whole section is."

Ally couldn't help but notice how her pile of presents was larger than the rest. "Wow! And you'll get even more presents from Santa, too."

"Yeah, I have a feeling she's not going to be wanting for anything this Christmas," Chase confirmed, coming up behind them.

"Who's got all these presents?" Cassie joining in the conversation.

"They're mine!" Fatima grinned from ear to ear.

Yours for the Holiday

"All yours? No way! That's a way bigger pile than mine. Do you know what's in them yet?"

"No! We're not supposed to open them until tomorrow," Fatima replied, as if she thought Cassie was being silly.

"Oh, well, that never stopped me and Ally from guessing what was in them on Christmas Eve," Cassie pointed out. "C'mon. Let's see if we can figure out what's in them."

Cassie gave Chase and Ally a wink, like she was doing the two of them a favour by taking Fatima off their hands and giving them some alone time. Ally wanted to roll her eyes at her but refrained because she knew her sister's heart was in the right place.

"Speaking of presents…" Chase pulled out a silver-and-black wrapped gift from his pocket and held it out to her. "I got you something."

"Chase, you shouldn't have. I feel bad that I didn't get you anything."

"You don't need to get me anything," he assured her. "This is just something small I found that I thought you might like to have."

She looked at him quizzically, but took the box from him.

"Go on," he said. "Open it. You don't need to wait. You're going to want it for the dance later." She unwrapped the long rectangular box and lifted the lid, revealing the charm bracelet that Chase had given all those years ago, the one she'd thought she'd lost.

"My bracelet! Where did you find it?"

"It must've fallen in behind one of the seats of the couch, or something, because I found it in my things when I was moving into Josh and Kayla's place after university."

She took the chain in her fingers and noticed a sapphire blue snowflake charm with white glitter. It had been the first charm Chase had ever given her. They'd been eight years old with their parents at a summer baseball game. While Ally had always like baseball, there was only so long an eight-year-old's attention could focus on one thing, and she'd decided she'd wanted a slushie, so their parents had given them some money and let them go to the concession stand just a few feet away. As they'd walked over to it, Chase had spied something in the dirt.

"What's this?" he'd knelt down to pick it up. It was the snowflake charm. "Here," he'd said, handing it to her. "It's your favourite colour. It'll be your lucky charm."

She'd taken it from him and had thought at the time that there had never been a prettier piece of jewellery than the cheap little snowflake charm. It had felt like he'd given her the most precious jewel in the world. From that night onwards, for every birthday and holiday, he'd given her a charm to add to her collection.

"Here, let me help you put it on." Chase delicately took her wrist in his hand and attached the bracelet. The metal felt cool against her skin. She smiled up at them, their eyes connecting for a brief moment.

"What do we have here?" Ally turned around at the sound of Kayla's voice behind her.

"No way! Is that the charm bracelet you thought you lost in senior year?" Kayla reached out for her wrist to have a better look at the bracelet.

"Chase just gave it to me. Said he found it in one of the couch cushions awhile ago or something." Ally smiled, pleased at having her favourite piece of jewellery back again.

"Did he now…" Kayla smirked at him as she admired the bracelet. "Well, I'm glad you got it back. I know how much it means to you."

"What are we all looking at?" Josh asked, joining their group after hanging up his and Kayla's jackets.

Yours for the Holiday

"Look, Josh. Chase found Ally's charm bracelet."

"Oh, nice." Josh glanced at the bracelet, but in typical guy form, he was dispassionate about it.

Kayla rolled her eyes at her fiancé. "Typical dude. C'mon, Ally. Let's leave these two to talk about something boring like hockey, or something."

"Oh, ok." Ally reluctantly let her whisk her away from Chase, looking back one last time at him before he disappeared into the crowds. She'd wanted to properly thank him for returning her bracelet to her.

"So?" Kayla asked, when she'd spirited Ally away to the den just off the kitchen. It was much quieter in here, away from the main action.

"So, what?" Ally asked, clueless.

"You've been holding out on me!" Kayla chastised, sitting down on the leather couch beside her.

"What do you mean?" Ally asked, not playing coy. She actually didn't know what she was talking about.

"Do you want to tell me something important, like something to do with a certain job in L.A.?" Kayla prodded, being a little more specific this time.

"Oh, my God! Yes! Of course, the role." Ally breathed a sigh of relief, finally catching onto what Kayla had been talking about.

"Yes, the role! I had to hear it from Josh that you got it."

"Yeah, sorry. It's just been a crazy busy, you know, with all the last-minute planning for the dance, and then telling my family about it..." She hoped she sounded sufficiently apologetic. She hadn't meant to *not* tell Kayla; she'd just forgotten in the excitement of it all.

"I forgive you, I suppose," Kayla teased, no hint of malice in her voice. "And I'm so thrilled for you! So, when do you start?"

"Actually, I have to leave the day after tomorrow,"

Ally conceded.

"So soon? But we just got you back here." Kayla's posture slumped delicately with disappointment. "What does this mean about Chase?"

"What do you mean?"

"Oh, come on, Al. He just happens to give you back your bracelet that he knows means so much to you after he finds out that you're going to leave, again? If that's not a gesture, I don't know what is."

Ally subconsciously touched the bracelet, the feel of its cold, smooth metal a reassuring presence now that it was back on her wrist. Kayla was right: there was undeniably some kind of spark still between the two of them, and she was feeling more than ever that Chase felt it too, even if the two of them hadn't admitted it out loud to each other yet.

"So, what are you going to do about it?" Kayla asked.

"I don't know," she replied honestly. "I never expected any of this when I came back home, and I certainly didn't expect it to happen so suddenly. I don't know how I feel about any of this."

"Well, you need to figure things out soon. It's not just Chase who's gotten attached." Kayla nodded towards the kitchen where Fatima had just entered. She smiled when she saw the two of them in the den. Ally knew she was concerned for the both of them; after all, they'd become family in the years since she'd been gone, and she was now on the outside of it all. Kayla was right: she needed to figure things out before she broke everyone's hearts, including her own.

"There you two are!"

"Oh, you found us!" Kayla teased her. "And we thought we were so clever, hiding in here."

"Chase says we need to get going if we're going to

Yours for the Holiday

make it to the nursing home in time to start the dance."

"Well, we better get a move on, then!" Ally stood up from the couch just as Mrs. Cormier was making an announcement from the kitchen.

"Alright, everyone! We're closing up for the night. Everyone is welcome to join us over at the nursing home to celebrate the rest of this party at the dance Chase, Fatima, and Ally have planned. So, let's get this show on the road!"

Everyone began moving in the direction of the door, gathering up their coats and boots.

"See you over there," Chase said, smiling at her.

"See you soon."

༺༻

Twenty minutes later, Ally walked into the rec room of the nursing home and gazed at all the hard work she and Chase had put into the place. It looked even more magical than she'd thought it would be.

"Oh my God." Cassie stood there in the entrance with her, gazing up at the sparkling snowflakes Chase had hung from the ceiling. "This place looks amazing! Wow, Ally; you've really outdone yourself."

"Well, she had help!" Fatima came up to them and joined the conversation, a big grin on her face.

"Yes, we did. We had the best helper." Chase smiled at her.

"This place looks... wow!" Ally stared in wonder at how well everything had come together.

Chase smiled at seeing her so happy. "Well, I couldn't have done it without you." She blushed under the glow of the Christmas lights. Subconsciously tucking a curl behind her ear.

"Oh! Don't you two look so lovely!" her grandmother shuffled over to them.

"Thanks, Grams. You look beautiful yourself." She noticed her grandmother had chosen a festive green gown to wear, with a silver locket her grandfather had given her for one of their wedding anniversaries.

"Oh, well." Her grandmother patted her curls, looking self-confident.

"Grams, would you do me the pleasure of having a dance with me?" Chase asked, holding his hand out to her.

"Well, how could I refuse such a request from such a handsome young man?" Ally's grandmother let herself be whisked away to the dancefloor by Chase. Ally watched as he expertly moved her around the dancefloor. She smiled once again at how good he was with people of all ages. Chase really was the perfect guy.

So, why are you letting him go again? her subconscious asked her.

"Whatcha looking at?" Kayla asked, coming up behind her, interrupting her thoughts.

"Nothing," she replied a little too quickly, turning away from Chase and her grandmother. Kayla gave her a pointed look, like she knew Ally wasn't telling her the truth, but she couldn't quite prove it just yet.

"This place is great," Josh said, joining them. "Thanks, Ally, for helping out and doing all this. I'm glad you were around to help."

"It was my pleasure," she replied, smiling.

"Hey Josh, Kayla. Look where you two are standing!" Fatima interrupted them. The three of them looked around, trying to figure out what she was getting at. Finally, she pointed to the ceiling where a piece of mistletoe was hanging.

"Well, look at that," Josh replied slyly. "I suppose

Yours for the Holiday

this is your doing?"

"Maybe…" Fatima replied, a big grin on her face. "Grams thought it would be a fun idea. She helped out."

"Oh, I bet she did," Ally chuckled. "And how many people have you ensnared in your little trap so far?"

"Oh, just Mr. and Mrs. Morris, so far." She nodded in the direction of an elderly couple sitting down at a nearby table.

"Well, I suppose we shouldn't break with tradition." He pulled Kayla in close, giving her a romantic kiss. A few whistles and some clapping erupted from the residents. Josh laughed and turned to Ally. "You were under here, too. Come on in for a smooch. Or maybe there's someone else you'd rather be kissing?"

She looked around at just that moment to see Chase and her grandmother joining them.

"Oh, no. I'm not going to fall for that. In fact, I'm going to go way over to the other side of the room, now, to stay away from that," she teased, pointing to the mistletoe.

"I think I'll join you," Chase said, following her out to the dancefloor.

They didn't hear Fatima as she leaned in to whisper to Grams, "They still don't know about the others we hung around the room."

Grams gave her a wink.

"Well, let's keep that between ourselves, for now," she said conspiratorially. "In fact, I have a good challenge for you. I bet you can't get those two under this mistletoe for a kiss before midnight."

Fatima's eyes took on a determined look. "Oh yeah? I'll take that bet," she replied, and headed off to put her plan into motion.

"What do you think those two are conspiring about?" Chase asked Ally as she checked in with some of the residents. She followed his gaze to Fatima and her grandmother.

"I don't know... but I'm willing to bet those two are up to something." Just then, the music changed from "Rockin' Around the Christmas Tree" to "O Holy Night."

"Care to dance?" Chase held his hand out to her. She felt her heart flutter. She knew she shouldn't do it, but she took his hand anyways.

"Sure."

He led her to the centre of the small dancefloor, the two of them not noticing the smiles and curious glances they were getting from the residents. For her, everything else in the world just faded away. The only thing that existed was the two of them, the feel of his strong shoulders as she rested her hands on them, the feel of his warm hands on the curve of her hips through the thin fabric of her dress. She leaned her head forward a bit, meeting him in the centre where he rested his chin against her skin. She closed her eyes, breathing him in, and for the first time in a very long time, she felt connected. They expertly glided around the dancefloor, almost as if they were one person, in total sync with one another. They were so wrapped up in one another that they hadn't noticed how the others dancing around them had been gently nudging them around the dancefloor to a specific spot.

All too soon, the music ended, and Ally reluctantly took a step back. She gazed up into his eyes, seeing the way he was looking at her.

"Thanks," she whispered, barely audible over the din of the room. "That was…"

"I know," he replied, not needing her to finish her sentence for him. "I…" he started to say, but the two of them were interrupted by Fatima.

"Look where you two are standing," she piped up. This time, they knew to look up at the ceiling.

"I do not remember hanging that there before," Ally said, her tone amused at seeing another branch of mistletoe conveniently hanging above them.

"Don't look at me," Chase replied, putting his hands up defensively. "I had nothing to do with this." Fatima and Ally's grandmother giggled like two little schoolkids.

"Exactly how many of these did you put up?" Ally asked them.

"Oh, just three or four," her grandmother replied, pointing them out around the room, overly pleased with herself.

"Well, Mr. Cormier, I believe we've been set up."

"I think you're right." Chase glanced at the two of them, as well as Josh, Kayla, and Cassie on the other side of the room. "It would seem that there's a number of people conspiring to get us under the mistletoe tonight."

"Well, it would be a shame to disappoint them," she said, surprising herself. Chase seemed just as surprised by the bold gesture.

"I suppose it would." He brought his face close to hers, pausing for only the briefest of seconds to get her consent before he kissed her.

Once again, the world around them faded: the music, the people; nothing else existed in those brief seconds except for the two of them. There was only her and him, the two of them as one. All too soon, they parted, and before she even opened her eyes, she knew everything had changed between them. Looking into his eyes now, she knew he felt it too.

"Umm…" she started.

"I should… go over… Yeah. Sorry." And with that, he took off across the room towards his office. Ally glanced around her, slightly bewildered, unsure of exactly how everything went from perfect to a perfect disaster in less than a minute. She looked at Kayla for advice, just as Josh took off in the same direction as Chase. The others regarded her sympathetically, like they weren't sure what had just happened, either.

"Should I...?"

"No. Josh has got it covered." Kayla took her by the shoulders. "Come on, let's get you a drink."

"I think I'm going to need something a little stronger than the fruit punch." Her cheeks were flushed red under the twinkly Christmas lights and she had the distinct feeling that everyone was staring at her. She just wanted to run and hide from them all.

"I know..." Kayla reached out and squeezed her hand. "I wish we could, but regulations." She shrugged.

"Yeah, I know. Oh, God! Why did I do that? I totally pressured him into that kiss. I should've just left things alone. Now I've ruined everything."

"No, sweetie, you didn't." It seemed like Kayla wanted to say more, but she wasn't sure if she should. "Look, Chase... this time of year is just hard for him and I'm sure there's just some things he needs to work through right now. I really don't think it has anything to do with you. Since you've been home, he's been the happiest he's been in a long time."

Ally knew she was trying to be reassuring, but it wasn't having the effect she intended.

"Ok, but what kind of things? I tried asking Mom and Cass about it the other day and all they told me was that they felt Chase should be the one to talk to me about it. What happened while I was away, Kayla?"

Kayla took a sip of her punch, burying her face in her cup. "I know you're not going to want to hear this, but I don't think it's my place to discuss it. I think it's something you should talk to Chase about. I'm sorry."

"No, I'm sorry. I shouldn't try to get involved.

Yours for the Holiday

Maybe it's a good thing I'm leaving early. I've gotten way more involved in his life again than I'd intended." She sipped away at her punch, trying to ignore the sympathetic glances her grandmother was giving her from across the room. For the rest of the night, she tried to put on a brave face.

They spent the rest of the dance on opposite sides of the room. She'd wanted to go over to him, to apologize for the kiss, but she'd held back, giving him his space. Sometime just before midnight, the dance wound down, many of the senior residents contentedly nodding off in their chairs. As the staff helped them back to their rooms and their families departed, Ally started cleaning up some of the mess.

"You can just leave that. The rest of the staff can clean the rest of it up tomorrow." She turned around at the sound of Chase's voice.

"I don't mind." In fact, the busy work helped keep her attention on something other than him.

"Do you want a lift home?"

She glanced around the room to find that they were the only two left. Cassie and her parents had taken off without her, and all the residents had returned to their rooms.

"Yeah, that'd be great. Thanks."

"No problem." He flipped his keys around on the fob nervously, making a jangling sound. She grabbed her coat and scarf from the chair she'd put it on earlier. Her fingers shook slightly as she tried to push the smooth plastic buttons into the right holes and she feared she'd do them up in the wrong order, but she managed to make herself presentable before heading out into the cold towards Chase's truck and the two of them headed home.

A light snow fell around them, glistening in the glow of the streetlights. The whole neighbourhood was so quiet it was possible to hear the snow as it fell. She and

Chase had driven the whole way home in silence, neither one of them sure what to say to one another after their kiss earlier. She almost regretted it now; it had changed everything between them. Before, they had skirted around their feelings and just keep up the old flirty banter between them without getting serious, but the kiss had changed the dynamic between them, and she found herself wanting to go back to before it had happened. She sat there in the passenger seat a moment too long. Just as she felt Chase was about to politely suggest she get out of the car, she made up her mind.

"Do you want to come inside for a bit? I've got something I want to show you." Her heart skipped a beat, then two, as she waited for him to respond.

"Ok." She could tell from his tone that he wasn't entirely comfortable with the idea, but there was also a feeling that maybe he wished they could just go back to how things were before, too. "What is it?"

"It's a surprise. Now, let's get inside before we freeze." He followed her inside, hesitating in the doorway for just a moment.

"Just leave your boots and coat down here. You can get them later. Now, hurry up before my parents see the light on." She didn't wait for him to follow; she just knew intuitively that he would follow her up the stairs.

When they were in her bedroom, she gestured for him to take a seat on her bed while she turned and began rummaging through her dresser drawer. Out of the corner of her eye, she could see him looking around her room, noticing how it hadn't changed since high school. She wondered if he was remembering the same memories she'd had of the two of them in this bedroom, memories of a lifetime of sleepovers and late-night study sessions where she did most of the studying, while he kind of just stared at her in awe and she pretended not to notice. Their whole lives –

minus the last six years – had been spent together, and a lot of that time had been spent in this very room. He appeared completely at home here, like he'd reclaimed a part of him that had been missing.

"Ah ha!" she exclaimed proudly, turning around. "Look what I found!"

Chase noticed her old MP3 player in her hand. He looked at her curiously. "Is that what I think it is?"

"Scootch over."

He acquiesced and moved over to make room for her on the bed. She held out one earbud for him to take, while she put in the other. She hit play and watched as his face lit up as he recognized the playlist she'd made it for him for their first day of high school to help calm his nerves about going to a new school. The two of them hummed quietly along with the music, the old familiarity of a shared life together helping them to relax again. She felt him move slightly onto his side, so he was facing her, their noses only centimetres apart from each other. Lost in the familiarity of being together, the two of them drifted off to sleep.

Chapter Eleven

She woke to the smell of coffee and breakfast cooking in the kitchen below her. She opened her eyes sleepily and her heart wanted to both swell with happiness and stop with fear when she saw Chase's face mere inches from hers. His face was relaxed in sleep, a slight curl of his mouth turned up into a small smile, like he was having a particularly good dream. She hated to wake him, but with the way the smell of breakfast was wafting up to her room, she knew it would only be moments before her mother or her sister would burst into her bedroom to wake her up.

"Chase!" she hissed at him, giving his shoulder a little shove. "Wake up! We've overslept!"

"Mmmm… wha—…?" he asked sleepily. Her heart was thrilled when she saw how his smile widened when his eyes focused on her face, but she knew that, as much as she might like to, she didn't have time to revel in

Yours for the Holiday

it.

"Get up! You have to get out!" She rose from the bed, throwing on a sweater over her dress, suddenly self-conscious about how she must look right now.

"You know, it's not like I haven't been having sleepovers in your bedroom since we were seven," he grumbled, locating the socks he'd kicked off sometime in the night.

"This isn't like when we were seven at all, and you know it!" she hissed at him.

"Well, how am I supposed to get my boots or my coat?" he finally asked her, looking down at his sock feet. He couldn't very well go downstairs to get to his stuff by the front door without the likelihood of at least someone in her family seeing him.

"You'll just have to go out the window," she said, coming to the only realization of how to get him out without anyone finding him here.

"In my sock feet?!"

"Keep your voice down!" she hissed at him again. "Someone'll hear you! You'll be fine; you live just across the driveway. It's only a few feet."

"Yeah, in the frickin' snow!" he hissed back at her as he made his way reluctantly to the window ledge. He pulled back the curtains and opened the window, letting in the sub-zero wind. She involuntarily shivered at the sudden drop in temperature.

"Now, climb out the window before anyone comes up here," she commanded.

"Fine, I'm doing it. See?" He manoeuvred his way out the window and down to the trellis. She leaned out the window, watching as he slowly worked his way down the cold latticework. When he was about halfway down, his foot slipped.

"Dammit!"

"Chase!" Her heart stopped in her chest. There was snow drift directly below him, so the possibility of him getting hurt was quite small, but still, it made her worry for his safety.

"I'm ok. I'm ok," he called up, pausing a moment.

"Chase? Is that you?" His mother opened up his old childhood bedroom across the driveway and peered out at them, Fatima joining her at the windowsill.

"Oh, hello Ally, dear," Mrs. Cormier called across the way. She raised an eyebrow at her slightly dishevelled appearance in last night's dress.

"Hello Mrs. Cormier!" she called out, trying in vain to stop her facing from blushing. She knew how this must look.

"Chase, dear, do get down from there before you break your neck. You're not a child anymore. You're too big to be climbing in and out of Ally's window. Just use the front door like a normal person."

"Yes, Mother. That had been the plan," he grumbled, looking up at Ally with an I-told-you-so look. She rolled her eyes at him. He was just a few feet from the ground now, and he jumped off the lattice, landing with a quiet thud into the snowbank below.

"Chase! I think you forgot these on your way out." Ally heard her mother open the kitchen window directly below and saw her hand Chase his coat and boots.

"Uh, thanks Mrs. Hayes." He smiled at her and gave a small wave as he took his things from her outstretched hands, Fatima giggling at him from the upstairs window.

"Now, get yourself home before your feet fall off from the cold," she scolded him.

"Will do, Mrs. Hayes." He turned to walk the few

Yours for the Holiday

feet to his parents' house.

"And Chase?"

"Yes, Mrs. Hayes?" He turned around to look at her.

"For heavens' sake, just use the front door next time."

"Sure thing, Mrs. Hayes. Merry Christmas!"

"Merry Christmas, dear." Ally put her face in her palm, knowing the litany of questions she was going to get when she went downstairs. "Ally? Now that Chase is gone, it's time for breakfast!"

"Yes, Mom! Be right down!" She descended the stairs, hoping her face wasn't beet red.

"A very Merry Christmas, dear," her mother gestured for her to take a seat with her father and sister at the dining room table, which was laden with the impressive Christmas breakfast she'd prepared.

"Merry Christmas, everyone." She settled herself at the table.

"And how's Chase this Christmas morning?" her grandmother asked, teasing her. "A little cold, I'd imagine, climbing down that old trellis in sub-zero temperatures in nothing but his sock feet."

Ally's face returned to its previously red hue. "I'm sure he's fine," she mumbled around a mouthful of toast. "And he was wearing more than that!"

"What's that dear?"

"Oh, come now. Let's not tease her. It's Christmas, after all. You'll have plenty of time to tease the two of them later today when the Cormiers come over for Christmas dinner."

Ally nearly choked on her piece of toast.

"Don't look so worried, sis. It's not like we're going to let you and Chase live this down for years to come,"

Cassie teased her. Ally put her head in her hands, trying to hide her face.

"Alright, enough teasing her," her mother said, this time more seriously. "Who wants to open presents?"

"I do!" Cassie replied quickly, bolting from the table to the Christmas tree in one second flat, reverting to her child-like self. They all laughed as they followed her out into the living room, bringing their breakfasts with them.

As Ally watched her sister tear her way through her presents, she couldn't help but feel a bit of apprehension settle into the pit of her stomach at the thought of seeing Chase again later today. Even though things between them had ended on a good note, she knew that there was still a lot of awkwardness between them after their kiss, which was only going to make getting through this Christmas dinner that much harder.

※

What Ally loved most about Christmas was the sense of community she felt when she was back in her old neighbourhood. She hadn't realized how much she'd missed that until she'd moved to Los Angeles. The other thing she loved about the holidays was the inclusion of traditional foods from all around the world. With four families coming from different backgrounds: Kayla's family being Filipino-Canadian, Josh's family being Irish, the Hayes family being English, and Chase's family having Acadian and Mi'kmaq heritage, there were traditional dishes from several countries and cultures. And now, she noticed as she stepped into the kitchen, they were adding Syrian food to the menu in honour of Fatima.

"Wow, that smells great!" she said, coming into the

kitchen. Her mother, grandmother, Cassie, Kayla, Fatima, and Chase were all in the kitchen.

"Chase and I are making kibbeh, baklava, seafood chowder, and bûche de Noël," Fatima said proudly, showing off her baklava.

"Wow! That looks so yummy. You made this all by yourself?"

"Well, Chase and Kayla helped a bit," Fatima admitted. "And now I'm helping Kayla to make her biko."

"You shared your mother's special recipe with her, but you won't teach me how to make your mother's biko?" Ally teased Kayla.

"Well, maybe if you showed some interest in cooking or baking, I would have," Kayla teased her back. Ally couldn't disagree with that argument.

"Well, can I help out now?"

"No offense, Al, but I think we have enough cooks in the kitchen," Cassie told her. With so many people in the kitchen, space was pretty limited.

"Alright, I'll just go and join the others." She was a bit relieved when she felt her phone buzzing in her pocket, giving her an excuse to get out of the busy kitchen.

"Hey Liv!" She opened her video chat to see her friend's excited face. "Merry Christmas!"

"It sure is a merry Christmas," Liv exclaimed, the snowy Vermont mountains in the background of her video setting the perfect tone for the festive day. Liv held her hand up to the screen to show off her new engagement ring.

"Is that…? Did he…?"

"Yup!" Liv's face broke out into an even bigger grin.

"Yay! I'm so excited for you!"

"I mean, let's be real. All the signs were there, and

we all kinda knew this was coming. Even so, I can't quite believe it! I just wish we kind of had more time here to enjoy our engagement before heading back to L.A. But it means I'll get to see you again!"

"I know what you mean," Ally said. "It's hard to believe that we have to be on set in two days. I can't wait to see that ring in person."

"Oh, come on. I know you had a hand in picking this out for me."

Ally gave her a sly grin. "Well, maybe just a little…" she admitted. "But I haven't seen it in person on your hand, and that's the most important thing."

"So, how's your Christmas going so far? Have you and Chase finally gotten together yet?" Ally felt a well of emotions at all the questions. There were so many things she had to tell Liv about the last twenty-four hours.

"Honestly, there's so much to tell you; too much to get into over the phone. But I promise we'll get into it when I see you tomorrow."

"Hmm… Everything ok?" Liv asked, her face taking on a concerned look, noticing Ally's muted expression.

"Yes and no," she admitted. "Look, we have guests over for Christmas dinner, so I promise I'll give you more details when I see you in person."

"Ok, well, if you need to talk about anything in the meantime, just call me."

"I promise, I will. Now, go on and enjoy your big day! Can't wait to see you!"

"Talk to you soon!"

Ally smiled and waved to her as she hung up the phone. Trying to tamp down her anxieties, she plastered on a cheerful smile and headed back out into the living room to join the others. A couple of hours later, Chase emerged from the kitchen. "Supper is just about ready if

Yours for the Holiday

you'd like to join us in the dining room."

The others rose and followed him in. Ally breathed in the scents of all the different foods laid out on the buffet table they'd set up along the far wall of the dining room. A long dining table had been set up in here and one in the living room with little name cards on all the seats, evenly dividing up the guests so there was a mixture of different age groups at each table.

Ally waited patiently in line for her turn, loading her plate up with turkey and vegetables, as well as the kibbeh that Chase and Fatima had made earlier, and some of Kayla's pancit. She made her way to the table, looking over the name cards, trying to find hers. Finally, she found it, conveniently placed right next to Chase. She glanced at her grandmother, who had a Cheshire cat grin on her face. Ally shook her head and rolled her eyes, but she knew her grandmother was only trying to get her and Chase to talk things over. She meant well, and she couldn't fault her for that. Dutifully, Ally took her seat.

"All packed?" he asked as she settled in. She could tell from the look on his face that he didn't want to be asking her this, but a lifetime of good manners wouldn't loosen their grip on him.

"Yeah, mostly. I never really unpacked, to tell you the truth. I wasn't planning on staying here long, in the first place."

"Right." She noticed his posture stiffen at the reminder. "What time do you head out?"

"First thing in the morning," she confirmed. "I'll basically be landing in L.A. and heading directly to set."

"Well, I hope you have a safe flight." He gave her a half-smile, taking a bite of his turkey. She wanted to say so much to him in this moment, to tell him she didn't want to leave him, or Fatima, to tell him how much she wanted to stay with the two of them and see where this was all headed. She wanted to tell him how this role wasn't as important to her as he was, even if it wasn't strictly true. She wanted both things: a life with him and her dream career, but she couldn't have both, not unless one of them was willing to compromise. And she couldn't ask him to uproot his and Fatima's life here, not to follow her out to Los Angeles for a career which may take off with this role or may not. Nothing in her line of work was stable, and the both of them needed that stability. But she never got to say any of this to him, for his attention then was turned by his father, who had asked him a question.

Before the dance, before the kiss, Ally had been kind of disappointed by the timing of this new role, no matter how great it was going to be for her career. Now, she wondered if maybe this wasn't all for the best. She wished that the hours between now and her flight tomorrow would just fly by so she could get back to Los Angeles and her life before everything seemed to get off track again. Everything was just less complicated there, and right now, uncomplicated sounded like exactly what she needed.

Chapter Twelve

Boxing Day

"Well, I guess this is it." Ally stood outside in the driveway, her suitcases loaded into the taxi, ready and waiting for her.

"Are you sure you don't want us to drive you to the airport?" her father asked.

"No, I'll be fine." Truth be told, she didn't think she'd get on the plane this time if everyone was there to see her off. She knew this role was a big opportunity for her, but it seemed harder to leave this time than it had before.

"Well, give us a hug, then." Her parents pulled her in for a light hug. "You make sure to call us the moment you land in L.A. to let us know you made it there safe and sound."

"I will, I promise." She let them go and turned towards her sister who, despite all her bravado, had tears in the corner of her eyes.

"I'll call every day," Ally reassured her.

"Sure, whatever," Cassie replied, like it was no big deal, but then flung her arms around her. "I enjoyed having you home," she whispered in her ear.

"I know."

"And if you ever tell anyone, I'll deny it."

"I'll miss you, too, Cass." Reluctantly, she turned away and leaned down to gently hug her grandmother.

"Now don't you go and fall down anymore while I'm gone," she admonished her, but there was no bite to her bark. "You do what the doctors tell you."

Her grandmother scoffed at her. "And what do those charlatans know?" Ally gave her a pointed look, but didn't argue. Without meaning to, her eyes drifted over to the Cormier house for a brief second. She thought she saw the curtain in Chase's old room move a bit, but she couldn't be sure. She was disappointed he wasn't here, but she didn't feel that she could blame him. If their roles were reversed, she couldn't say that she wouldn't have stayed away, too.

"I thought he'd be here, too," her grandmother whispered in her ear.

"Well, I should get going. Don't want to miss that flight." She rose from her crouched position and headed over to the taxi, opening the back door and getting inside before she had the chance to change her mind. As the cab pulled out into the street, she waved to her family and gave one last look back at Chase's house, her heart still hoping he'd show up and ask her to stay.

Yours for the Holiday

Two months later...

"Hey you." Kayla's voice brought him out of his reverie as he stood in front of the washer and dryer.

"Oh, hey! Didn't see you there." He rearranged his expression, hoping his face wouldn't betray the fact that he'd been thinking about Ally. He'd done that a lot in the couple of months since she'd left; even though she wasn't here, she still seemed to have a hold over him.

"Laundry day?" she asked, making small talk.

"Yeah. I don't know how she does it, but Fatima seems to go through every piece of clothing in her closet in a single day," he replied.

"Just wait until she's a teenager," Kayla chuckled. An uncomfortable pause fell between them. "So… How are things? How have you been…?" Her voice trailed off like she wanted to say something more specific but was afraid to.

He knew what she wanted to ask him. He'd been in pain ever since he'd watched Ally get into that taxi and head to the airport. It had been too painful to watch her go, even though he'd known there was nothing he could have said to make her stay. She'd gotten that big role, and he knew in his heart of hearts that no matter how much he wanted to run out to her and convince her to stay here with him, he couldn't be the one to take her dreams away from her. So, just like he'd done six years ago when she'd first left for Los Angeles, he'd ended up just watching her from his childhood bedroom window, hoping beyond hope that she'd change her mind. In the months since, he'd been trying to hide his pain from everyone around him, but he was beginning to suspect that he hadn't been as good at it as he'd thought.

"Ok, I'm just going to come out and say this. I may be overstepping here, but I've seen how you've been since Ally left, Chase, and maybe... maybe you should tell her about Samar." Kayla stood before him, an exasperated and sympathetic look on her face.

"I'm not sure what that would accomplish," he said, loading in another pile of clothes, trying not to look her in the eye. "She's gone. We're in her rearview mirror. Who knows when we'll see her again?"

Kayla pursed her lips and pressed forward. "Ally thinks that the reason you pulled away after your kiss on Christmas Eve is because of her, because of how things went down between the two of you the first time she left for L.A. She thinks this whole situation is her fault."

Chase finally looked up at her, his eyebrows knitting together in a confused frown. "She didn't say anything about that. Not Christmas Eve, or at the dinner on Christmas Day." In fact, she'd barely spoken two words to him on Christmas Day. He'd thought that after his escapade getting out of her room that morning practically in front of the whole neighbourhood, that the two of them would at least have had something to talk about with where things were going with them, but they'd only exchanged small talk about her leaving.

"Of course not." Kayla crossed her arms across her chest. "No one told her about Samar, because we all thought it was best coming from you. All she knows is that you suddenly have a ten-year-old living with you, and something bad happened to you while she was away. I know that she knows the two things are related because

Yours for the Holiday

Fatima told me she took Ally through your part of the house where all Samar's stuff still is, but because we were all waiting for you to talk to her about it, none of us explained who Fatima is to you. And, Ally being Ally, she didn't want to make you feel bad because she was worried that she'd hurt you by asking for more details, but I think it's time you told her about the real reason why you pulled away that night, about how Ally's the first girl you've shown an interest in, let alone kissed, since Samar died. There's so much you haven't told her, and I understand you needed time to find the right way to explain things to her, but this has all gone on a little too long, now, don't you think? You're clearly miserable here without her, and Fatima misses her, too."

Chase let this information sink in. Had he been so blind not to notice that Ally had been as torn up about all this as he'd been?

Kayla delicately folded her arms across her chest. "I know that maybe none of this is my business, but I think you should at least tell her how you feel about her. You're still in love with her, and I'm pretty sure she feels the same way about you."

Chase's head whipped up at this. "You mean that? Did she say anything to you?" If Ally was going to reveal any feelings she had for him, Kayla was the first person she'd go to.

"Not exactly," Kayla admitted. "But I've known Ally my whole life, just like you, and I can still read her the same way I can read you. There's still something between the two of you, and I think you need to tell her how you feel."

Chase paused a moment, thinking about what to do with this information. After a brief moment, he said,

"Would you and Josh mind watching Fatima for me?"

"Of course, not." She waved her hand dismissively.

"No, I mean, like, for a few days?" He stared her right in the eyes this time, and he could see that she could tell where he was going with this.

"What exactly are you up to?" A curious look came across her face.

"I think I need to go on a road trip."

Chapter Thirteen

Valentine's Day

Sitting on the set of her new movie, Ally couldn't help but feel like something was missing. Ever since she'd come back to Los Angeles to begin filming, she'd felt like it went deeper than simply missing home. She just couldn't put her finger on it.

"Hey there! Penny for your thoughts?" Liv asked, joining her with her script in hand. The two of them were supposed to be going over their lines before their next scene, but Ally couldn't seem to focus on memorizing her new dialogue.

"Hey there!" She made an effort to put on her best smile for her. "It's nothing, just trying to memorize these new lines."

"I know you too well for that," Liv said, putting

down her script and getting straight to her point. "That isn't your 'studying my lines' face. That's your 'thinking about Chase' face."

Ally knew she'd been found out. "I don't know what you mean.

"Yes, I do. So, stop pretending and talk to me about it."

"How can you tell?"

"The way you get those little frowny lines on your forehead." Liv playfully poked her forehead, right where Ally could feel a frown forming. "Why don't you just pick up the phone and call him?"

"Because he doesn't want to talk to me."

"Based on what?"

"Uh, well, there's the fact that he literally bolted from the room after we kissed on Christmas Eve, then there's the fact that he didn't talk to me the whole way through Christmas dinner, and the fact that he hasn't once called me or messaged me, or even added me on social media since I came back here. If that isn't a sign that he wasn't interested in me, or in keeping in touch, I don't know what is."

Liv rolled her eyes. "I'm not convinced that was what he was thinking. You were the one who told me that the two of you were having a great time together right up until that kiss. And then the two of you had the uber cute sleepover, which you claim was totally innocent."

"Because it was! There was no removal of any clothing, despite where your mind is going," Ally exclaimed.

Liv laughed, but returned to her point. "I don't know… from what you've told me, it sounds like maybe he just got a little cold feet after the kiss, you know? I mean, how many girls has he dated since you two were together

Yours for the Holiday

in high school?"

"I don't know," she admitted. There was still so much she didn't know about his life from those years she'd been gone.

"And you said that you told him about Tom, right?"

"Yeah." Both of them unconsciously looked over at Tom's trailer. Of all the bad luck in the world, it had just so happened that he'd been cast opposite Liv as the male romantic lead. Ally had certainly not envied her having to act like she was in love with the jerk.

"So, maybe he's got stuff going on in his life, and with you having just got out of a relationship, maybe it all was just a little sudden for him. Guys are surprisingly sensitive that way, sometimes."

"Maybe you're right," Ally conceded.

"I think there's still something going on between you two and you should call him and ask him how he felt about that kiss instead of just speculating about it."

Liv handed her phone to her. "Go on. Call him."

"Don't you have a bunch of wedding decisions to think about? Or a scene to prepare for instead of bugging me about Chase?" Ally's tone was sharper than she'd meant it to be.

"I'm a multi-tasker. I can worry about multiple things as once," Liv teased her. A silence fell between them as they watched the hustle and bustle of the crew setting up the next scene. Just then, the last person Ally wanted to see was standing in front of her.

"Hello, ladies." Tom said, joining them. "Practicing your lines?"

"Don't you have somewhere else you could be right now?" Liv asked him, her tone openly hostile. She may have to pretend to be in love with him on screen, but that didn't mean that she and Ally had to put up with him when the cameras weren't rolling. "Don't you have a girlfriend or two you could be bothering right now instead of us?"

"Ah, come now, Livvie. Don't be like that." Tom stretched out his long legs, making himself even more comfortable in his chair, indicating he was going nowhere anytime soon. "Why the sour face, Al? What's your problem today?"

"You're my problem," she muttered.

"Oh, come now. We've been working together for a couple of months. Can't we put that whole Hawaii thing behind us? I'm sorry I took what's-her-name on the trip you and I were supposed to go on, but that was months ago. Can't we just move forward?"

"Charming. You can't even remember your ex-girlfriend's name. Remind me again what it was that I ever thought I saw in you?" Ally asked, seriously. Tom's smile faltered slightly.

"Ally?" one of the personal assistants tentatively approached the three of them, interrupting their conversation.

"What's up, Gina?" She always tried to make an effort to get to know everyone's names to show them she appreciated them, unlike her ex-boyfriend, who went through personal assistants almost as quickly as he went through girlfriends.

"There's a guy at the front gate of the lot who's insisting that he needs to see you. He says he's an old friend of yours… a Chase Cormier?"

Ally and Liv exchanged looks. "Yeah, I know him. You can tell security to let him in." She rose from her chair and followed Gina through the busy lot to where Chase was standing with a couple of security guards.

Yours for the Holiday

"Chase? What are you doing here?" She couldn't help how her face broke out into a big smile at the sight of him. Instantly, her mood was lifted and everything she thought she'd been missing before seemed to fade away.

"Ally!" His smile matched hers. "Hey."

"Hey." She couldn't believe he was really here, standing in front of her. In her dreams, she'd hoped that one day Chase might show up on in Los Angeles to see her, but they'd been just that: dreams. She reached out and touched his arm, as if to make sure he was real.

"I need to talk to you." Suddenly, his face became serious. "Is there somewhere we can talk?"

"Yeah, sure." She pulled him to the side a bit, away from the crowd. Taking his hand, she led him through the maze of the lot to her trailer. Once they were inside, she suddenly wondered if this had been the best idea. The place was small and cramped, and she was forced to stand quite close to him.

"How have you been?" She tried to casually lean against the countertop, still feeling as awkward as if she was meeting him for the first time.

"I'm good. Better, now, that I can see you." He smiled down at her, and she felt her heart flutter a bit. She still wasn't entirely sure this was all real. "I wanted to talk to you about the kiss we had on Christmas Eve," he blurted out, taking her by surprise.

"I'm sorry about that. I should've never pressured you into it. I should've known that it would dredge up all these horrible memories of the two of us, and that it would just end up hurting you, especially with me coming here to start filming so soon after I got back home…"

She dropped her head, staring down at the floor, afraid to look up at him. Suddenly, she felt one of his fingers under her chin, gently lifting her head.

"No, Ally, you have it wrong." His voice was low and husky. She mustered up the courage to look into his deep brown eyes, like dark pools sucking her in.

"I do?"

He nodded slowly. "The kiss... it changed things between us, yes, but I need you to know that I wasn't upset with you for it or anything like that. I was surprised you suggested it, but I was glad for it." She could see in his eyes that he was being sincere. Even so, she needed to hear him say it again.

"You were?"

He smiled. "Yeah... I mean, I'd been wanting to do that since the moment you came to the nursing home to visit your grandmother. I just didn't have the courage."

Ally breathed a sigh of relief. "But you avoided me the rest of the night, and then at dinner the next day you practically pretended I didn't exist, even though I was sitting there right next to you."

Chase broke his gaze from hers. "I know... I'm sorry. Things were... things are... complicated," he started.

"Because of Fatima?"

He nodded. "You see, it's different this time. It's not just me I have to think about. If it had been just me and my heart, then maybe I would've been willing to just have a fling with you over the holidays..."

Ally shook her head slightly. "You've never been that kind of guy, Chase."

He sighed, and she could feel his body relaxing next to hers. "Yeah, I guess you're right."

"It's not a bad thing, you know. In fact, it's one thing that I've always found most charming about you."

"Yeah?" he asked, a slight flush rising in his tanned cheeks.

"Yeah," she confirmed. She wanted so badly right now to reach up and take his face in her hands and kiss him, but she could sense that he had more to say.

"Anyways, it's not just me I have to consider now. There's Fatima, too, but that's only part of it." She stood there quietly, giving him the time to formulate the words he needed.

"After you left for L.A. the first time, I was devastated, and for a long time, I didn't think I was ever going to get over you." A part of her would have been lying if she'd said she hadn't been a little pleased to hear this admission from him. She'd never wanted to cause him any pain, but knowing that she wasn't that easy to get over was still more than a little satisfying to her ego.

"I thought there wasn't going to be anyone else for me, until suddenly, there was."

She nodded. She'd figured out this much on her own already. Still, hearing it from him, she wasn't sure how she felt about him being with someone else, especially if that person had been someone that Chase could have had a future with. She knew he hadn't been a monk in the six years since she'd left, but she'd also really not wanted to think of the possibility of Chase having been with other women.

"My life the last six years didn't exactly go the way I thought it would. I take it from Kayla that Fatima showed you our part of the house?"

She nodded. She hadn't wanted to press him about the woman in the photos or how he was connected to Fatima, but a part of her was dying to know the answers to the questions she had.

"So, you saw the pictures, then?" He seemed sad when she nodded, confirming his fears.

"I should've told you right from the start… I don't

know why I kept it all to myself. I guess I just didn't know how to bring it up and I was afraid of how it would change things, how it would change us."

"It's ok. I didn't want to press you about it, either." She crossed her arms across her chest in a self-protective move, knowing the worst was yet to be revealed.

He looked at her gratefully. "Her name was Samar. She and Fatima were originally from Syria. Her husband was killed when they tried to flee the civil war over there. Samar, her parents, and Fatima fled to a refugee camp in Jordan, where they stayed for several years. Her parents… they died there."

"That's terrible," Ally said quietly, feeling a sudden wave of sympathy for Fatima, only able to guess at the amount of pain and conflict she must have seen in her short life.

Chase took a deep, shaky breath. "Eventually, she and Fatima were granted asylum to come to Canada. Samar was trained as a nurse, you see, working in geriatrics, but since her credentials weren't recognized here, she had to re-train all over again. She started working as an orderly in the nursing home because she said that at least she could still care for the elderly, even if it wasn't exactly in the way she'd originally planned. That's where we met. I'd just started working there and literally bumped into her on my first day."

She watched his face as he smiled at the memory and felt both joy at seeing him happy, but a little sad that it had been because of someone else other than her.

"And then, of course, when I met Fatima… well, I knew then… I just knew that we were meant to be a family."

Ally couldn't help but smile along with him. But then his face clouded over and her chest constricted.

Yours for the Holiday

"Samar and I had just gotten engaged, and I'd just completed the paperwork to adopt Fatima when Samar was killed in a car accident only a couple of weeks after Christmas."

Ally felt her heart drop in her chest. That had been the reason she'd never seen Samar with Chase or Fatima the whole time she'd been home, why both Cassie and her mother had said that Chase should be the one to tell her the story himself, why Kayla had been protective of Ally getting too close to Chase and Fatima while she'd been home. Kayla had lost her mother when she'd only been a bit older than Fatima was now and knew all too well the hurt it had caused her. Ally couldn't imagine what it must have felt like to watch someone else go through the same thing.

"It was just one of those freak accidents," Chase continued, bringing her out of her thoughts. "The other driver hit a patch of black ice as she was coming home from work and slammed head first into her car. There was nothing anyone could've done. It was just one of those things."

She could see the tears forming at the corners of his eyes that he was trying to fight back.

"I'm so sorry, Chase." She reached over and hugged him tightly, trying to envelop him in her reassurance. There was nothing she could do to make this easier for him, she knew, but she hoped that just being here might give him some kind of comfort.

"Thanks," he said. A few minutes later, his voice was thick with emotion. "I think that's why planning the dance meant so much to Fatima. She has a way with the residents, just like her mother did, and I think she finds this time of year so hard to deal with, so she made a big deal about this dance as a way to cope with it all."

Ally nodded, understanding completely.

"And then when she met you, well, I haven't seen her that excited about meeting someone in a long time." He grinned at her. "And when the three of us were together, I just couldn't help but feel how natural it was between us, how well she took to you, and how well you took to her."

"Well, it's hard not to fall in love with that kid," Ally admitted.

"It's more than that. You make a great mom." He looked at her seriously now, and Ally felt a flush rise in her cheeks, embarrassed by the compliment. She hadn't thought of herself as the mothering type before, but when it had been the three of them, there had been a small part of her that had wondered what it would be like for them to be a family. "Well, she makes it look easy."

"That she does," he nodded. "Anyways, the night of the dance, I knew that, despite everything I'd done to set the right expectations, that she'd gotten her hopes up about the two of us getting back together. And even though I knew that, that was what I hoped for, I didn't want to impose my feelings or my life onto you, especially after you got this great part you've been waiting on for so long."

He gestured around to the busy set just beyond the door of her trailer, actors and crew milling about, setting up their scenes. "But more than that, it was the first time that I'd kissed anyone since… Samar passed… And I had a lot of feelings about that at the time that I just couldn't express without getting into everything."

Ally squeezed his hand. "You have nothing to be afraid of. Fatima's a great kid. You and Samar did a great job raising her, and, if you'd let me, I'd like to help continue with that."

Yours for the Holiday

Chase's head whipped up at this, his eyes searching her face like he wasn't quite sure if he'd heard what he'd just heard. "Do you mean that?"

"I do." She hadn't known she was going to say it until she did, but she felt it with a certainty she'd rarely experienced before. She just knew down to her core that she and Chase, and Fatima, belonged together as a family. The two of them had been the thing she'd been missing from her life since she'd left two months ago.

"But what about acting? You can't just give up on it now that everything's coming together for you."

"I didn't say it was going to be easy… I don't know how we're going to make it work, but I just know that we've got to try. I felt it that first time I saw you again, too. You and I belong together, Chase, and I couldn't imagine a better stepdaughter than Fatima. So, this is me standing here right now, saying: let's make this thing work this time."

Chase's face exploded into the biggest smile, the kind that she hadn't seen on him for years and it made her feel the happiest she'd been for a very long time. For the first time in a long time, she felt like everything in her life was exactly the way it was meant to be.

"Here." She turned around, opened her mini fridge, and took out two bottles of water. "I know it's not champagne or anything…"

"It's perfect," Chase reassured her.

"To us." She tipped her bottle towards his and took a sip.

"To us. Forever, this time."

Did you like *Yours for the Holiday*? Leave a review!

Yours for the Holiday can be found on the review site of your choice.

Read more from Erin Bowlen:

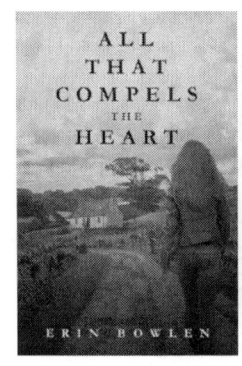

The Aoife O'Reilly series is a collection of bestselling women's fiction novels from Canadian author, Erin Bowlen. With its deeply drawn characters and slow-burn chemistry, you'll love this moving journey. Click the images above to begin reading now!

Made in the USA
Middletown, DE
14 May 2024